'Robustly brilliant ... This collection will provide manna to his admirers, and serve as the perfect introduction for those who have yet to discover his obsessive world.'

Daily Telegraph

'I love the work of Don DeLillo ... These nine pieces add up to something considerable, and form a vital addition to the corpus ... Very broadly, we read fiction to have a good time — though this is not to deny that the gods have equipped DeLillo with the antennae of a visionary. There is right field, and there is left field. He comes from third field — aslant, athwart. And I love *The Angel Esmeralda: Nine Stories*.'

Martin Amis, *New Yorker*

'Don DeLillo's richly compressed short stories are the work of a true master ... In these stories or lucid dreams — sometimes drily shocking or mournfully funny, always masterfully designed — DeLillo himself isolates that stray thought, and makes of it great art.'
Guardian

'Don DeLillo is a connoisseur of chaos. His authorial stance, if he may be said to have one, to the disasters peculiar to our time is that of a witness, bemused, detached, finical ... DeLillo is disruptively and subtly, even surreptitiously, funny ... a marvellous conceit, alarming and funny, a piece of vintage DeLillo bang up-to-date.'   John Banville, *Financial Times*

'Reading *The Angel Esmeralda* reminded me why DeLillo is a genius, and made me optimistic about whatever he writes next.'
Scotland on Sunday

'Written over thirty years, these stories evoke the same sense of pervasive alienation and dread DeLillo conjured in such masterful novels as *White Noise* and *Underworld* ... It is a measure of DeLillo's artistry that he makes the reader feel that this transitory moment of sublimity and grace will provide the watchers with enough redemption to make it through another day.'

Sunday Times

'The profundities and quandaries of existence weigh down mightily upon the shoulders of his characters and leave little room for any glimpses of joy. But for the reader, there is much pleasure to be gained from plunging headlong into the physical and psychological mazes within a DeLillo story and in *The Angel Esmeralda* we get a taste of his career's epic span with nine tales plucked from 1979's "Creation" up to this year's "The Starveling".'

The List

'If DeLillo's fiction has often, in the past, put us at the epicentre of historical events, looking over the shoulder of J. Edgar Hoover or Lee Harvey Oswald, these stories are attuned instead to more private terrors and tremors. They are gauges of a very fine precision, calibrated to detect the shocks of distant crises in the lives of people here and now.'

Literary Review

'DeLillo writes a highly stylised prose that marries a clean, chilly style to a kind of mysticism. This is a highwire combination ... at their heart these stories have the irresistible, unsolvable riddle of being alive in the world.'

The Times

'It is the perfect introduction to his themes and style. It is, unusually, his first collection of short stories after fifteen novels, and brings together work from the 1980s to the present. It is his entire career in miniature, and the later stories show that his talent is undiminished ... But if there were just a single story I'd give to a DeLillo sceptic, it would be "Midnight In Dostoevsky".'
Scotsman

'In gentler times than ours the US writer Don DeLillo would be respectfully acknowledged as a literary soothsayer. But it is now, and he is a witness of the moment, albeit a witness who saw it all coming long before everyone else did—with the honourable exception of the great J. G. Ballard ... Philip Roth in late career became the chronicler of the United States; Don DeLillo, however, has long been his country's wisest seer.'
Irish Times

'Both a terrific introduction to Don DeLillo if you've yet to dabble and a tremendously satisfying summation of what makes DeLillo great for the hardcore fan, this is an unmissable book.'
Bookmunch

'No other book has made me seriously think about the nature and purpose of fiction more than this collection of nine stories. Collated from over three decades, these chart DeLillo's trajectory, map out his themes and shine a light on some of the best prose written in this and the last century.'
Stuart Evers, Dirty / Realistic blogspot

'Pure grace and power.'
Catholic Herald

THE ANGEL ESMERALDA

NINE STORIES

Don DeLillo, the author of fifteen novels, including
Point Omega, *Falling Man*, *White Noise* and *Libra*, has
won many honours in America and abroad, including the
National Book Award, the PEN/Faulkner Award for Fiction,
the Jerusalem Prize for his complete body of work and the
William Dean Howells Medal from the American Academy
of Arts and Letters for his novel *Underworld*. In 2010,
he received the PEN/Saul Bellow Award.
He has also written three plays.

Novels

Americana

End Zone

Great Jones Street

Ratner's Star

Players

Running Dog

The Names

White Noise

Libra

Mao II

Underworld

The Body Artist

Cosmopolis

Falling Man

Point Omega

Plays

The Day Room

Valparaiso

Love-Lies-Bleeding

THE ANGEL ESMERALDA

NINE STORIES

DON DELILLO

PICADOR

First published 2011 by Scribner,
a division of Simon and Schuster, Inc., New York

First published in Great Britain 2011 by Picador

First published in paperback 2012 by Picador
an imprint of Pan Macmillan, a division of Macmillan Publishers Limited
Pan Macmillan, 20 New Wharf Road, London N1 9RR
Basingstoke and Oxford
Associated companies throughout the world
www.panmacmillan.com

ISBN 978-1-4472-0756-6

These stories appeared in the following publications: "Creation" in *Antaeus* 33, Spring
1979; "Human Moments in World War III" in *Esquire*, July 1983; "The Runner" in
Harper's, September 1988; "The Ivory Acrobat" in *Granta* 25, Autumn 1988; "The Angel
Esmeralda" in *Esquire*, May 1994; "Baader-Meinhof" in *The New Yorker*, April 1, 2002;
"Midnight in Dostoevsky" in *The New Yorker*, November 30, 2009; "Hammer and Sickle"
in *Harper's*, December 2010; and "The Starveling" in *Granta* 117, Autumn 2011.

The image on p. 45 is from the book *Herakleion Museum*, published by Ekdotike
Athenon, and is used with permission. The image on p. 103 is a painting by Gerhard
Richter and is used with permission of the Marian Goodman Gallery. Digital Image
© The Museum of Modern Art / Licensed by SCALA / Art Resource, NY.

1 3 5 7 9 8 6 4 2

A CIP catalogue record for this book is available from
the British Library.

Printed and bound by CPI Group (UK) Ltd, Croydon, CR0 4YY

Visit **www.picador.com** to read more about all our books
and to buy them. You will also find features, author interviews and
news of any author events, and you can sign up for e-newsletters
so that you're always first to hear about our new releases.

THE ANGEL
ESMERALDA

NINE STORIES

CONTENTS

PART ONE

Creation (1979)

Human Moments in World War III (1983)

CREATION

It was an hour's drive, much of it a climb through smoky rain. I kept my window open several inches, hoping to catch a fragrance, some savor of aromatic shrubs. Our driver slowed down for the worst parts of the road and the tightest turns and for cars coming toward us through the haze. At intervals the bordering vegetation was less thick and there were views of pure jungle, whole valleys of it, spread between the hills.

Jill read her book on the Rockefellers. Once into something she was unreachable, as though massively stunned, and all the way out I saw her raise her eyes from the page only once, to glance at some children playing in a field.

There wasn't much traffic in either direction. The cars coming toward us appeared abruptly, little color cartoons, ramshackle and bouncing, and Rupert, our driver, had to maneuver quickly in the total rain to avoid collisions and deep gashes in the road and the actual jungle pressing in. It seemed to be understood that any evasive action would have to be taken by our vehicle, the taxi.

The road leveled out. Now and then someone stood in the trees, looking in at us. Smoke rolled down from the heights. The car climbed again, briefly, and then entered the airport, a series of small buildings and a runway. The rain stopped.

I paid Rupert and we carried the luggage into the terminal. Then he stood outside with other men in sport shirts, talking in the sudden glare.

The room was full of people, luggage and boxes. Jill sat on her suitcase, reading, with our tote bags and carry-ons placed about her. I pushed my way to the counter and found out we were wait-listed, numbers five and six. This brought a thoughtful look to my face. I told the man we'd confirmed in St. Vincent. He said it was necessary to reconfirm seventy-two hours before flight time. I told him we'd been sailing; we were in the Tobago Cays seventy-two hours ago — no people, no buildings, no phones. He said it was the rule to reconfirm. He showed me eleven names on a piece of paper. Physical evidence. We were five and six.

I went over to tell Jill. She let her body sag into the luggage, a stylized collapse. It took her a while to finish. Then we carried on a formal dialogue. She made all the points I'd just made talking to the man at the counter. Confirmed in St. Vincent. Chartered yacht. Uninhabited islands. And I repeated all the things he'd said to me in reply. She played my part, in other words, and I enacted his, but I did so in a most reasonable tone of voice, and added plausible data, hoping only to soothe her exasperation. I also reminded her there was another flight three hours after this one. We'd still get to Barbados in time for a swim before dinner. And afterward it would be cool and starry. Or warm and starry. And we'd hear surf rumbling in the distance. The eastern coast was known for rumbling surf. And the following afternoon we'd catch our plane to New York, as scheduled, and nothing would be lost except several hours in this authentic little island airport.

"How neo-romantic, and how right for today. These planes seat, what, forty?"

"Oh, more," I said.

"How many more?"

"Just more."

"And we are listed where?"

"Five and six."

"Beyond the more than forty."

"Plenty of no-shows," I said. "The jungle swallows them up."

"Nonsense. Look at these people. They're still arriving."

"Some are seeing the others off."

"If he believes that, God, I don't want him on my side. The fact is they shouldn't be here at all. It's off-season."

"Some of them live here."

"And we know which ones, don't we?"

The plane arrived, from Trinidad, and the sound and sight of it caused people near the counter to push in more closely. I went around to the side and approached from behind the adjacent counter, where several others stood. The reconfirmed passengers began filing toward the immigration booth.

Voices. A British woman said the late-afternoon flight had been canceled. We all pushed in closer. Two West Indian men up front waved their tickets at the clerk. There were more voices. I jumped up several times in order to look over the heads of the assembled people to the dirt road outside. Rupert was still there.

Things were rapidly taking shape. Freight and luggage out one door, passengers out the other. I realized we were down to standbys. The people leaving the counter seemed propelled by some deep saving force. A primitive baptism might have been in progress. The rest of us crowded around the clerk. He was putting checks next to some names, cross-ing out others.

"The flight is full," he said. "The flight is full."

There were eight or ten faces left, bland in their travel-er's woe. Various kinds of English were being spoken. Some-one suggested we all get together and charter a plane. It was fairly common practice here. Someone else said something about a nine-seater. The first person took names, then went out with several others to find the charter office. I asked the clerk about the late-afternoon flight. He didn't know why it had been canceled. I asked him to book Jill and me on the first flight out next day. The passenger list wasn't available, he said. All he could do was put us on standby. We would all know more in the morning.

Using only feet, Jill and I pushed our luggage to the door. One of the charter prospects came back to tell us a plane might be available later in the day—a six-seater, only. This seemed to leave us out. I gestured to Rupert and we started taking things out to the car. Rupert had a long face and a gap between his front teeth and wore a silver medal over his breast pocket—an elaborate oval decoration attached to a multicolored strip of cloth.

Jill sat in back, reading. Out by the trunk, Rupert was say-ing he knew a hotel not far from the harbor. His gaze kept straying to the right. A woman was standing five feet away, very still, waiting for us to finish talking. I thought I recalled having seen her at the edge of the crowd inside the terminal. She wore a gray dress and carried a handbag. There was a small suitcase at her feet.

"Please, my taxi went back," she said to me.

She was pale, with a soft plain face, a full mouth and

cropped brown hair. She held her right hand up near her forehead to keep the sun out of her eyes. It was agreed we would share the taxi fare to the hotel and then ride out together in the morning. She said she was number seven.

It was hot and bright all the way back. The woman sat up front with Rupert. At intervals she turned to Jill and me and said, "It is awful, awful, the system they have," or, "I don't understand how they survive economically," or, "They could not guarantee I will get out even tomorrow."

When we stopped for some goats, a woman came out of the trees to sell us nutmeg in little plastic bags.

"Where are we listed?" Jill said.

"Two and three this time."

"What time's the flight?"

"Six forty-five. We have to be there at six. Rupert, we have to be there at six."

"I take you."

"Where are we going now?" Jill said.

"Hotel."

"I know hotel. What sort of hotel?"

"Did you see me jump, back there?"

"I missed that."

"I jumped in the air."

"It won't be Barbados, will it?" she said.

"Read your book," I told her.

The ketch was still anchored in the harbor. I pointed it out to the woman up front and explained that we'd spent the last week and a half aboard. She turned and smiled wanly as if she were too tired to work out the meaning of my remarks. We were in the hills, heading south. I realized what made this harbor town seem less faded and haphazard than the other small ports we'd put into. Stone buildings. It was almost Mediterranean.

At the hotel there was no problem getting rooms. Rupert said he'd be waiting at five next morning. Two maids preceded us along the beach, with a porter following. We split into two groups, and Jill and I were led to what was called a pool suite. Behind a ten-foot wall was a private garden of hibiscus, various shrubs and a silk-cotton tree. The small pool was likewise ours. On the patio we found a bowl full of bananas, mangoes and pineapple.

"Not half bad," Jill said.

She slept awhile. I floated in the pool, feeling the uneasy suspense lift off me, the fret of getting somewhere in groups—documented travel. This spot was so close to perfect we would not even want to tell ourselves how lucky we were, having been delivered to it. The best of new places had to be protected from our own cries of delight. We would hold the words for weeks or months, for the soft evening when a stray remark would set us to recollecting. I guess we believed, together, that the wrong voice can obliterate a landscape. This sentiment was itself unspoken, and one of the sources of our attachment.

I opened my eyes to the sight of wind-driven clouds— clouds *scudding*—and a single frigate bird hung on a current of air, long wings flat and still. The world and all things in it. I wasn't foolish enough to think I was in the lap of some primal moment. This was a modern product, this hotel, designed to make people feel they'd left civilization behind. But if I wasn't naive, I wasn't in the mood, either, to stir up doubts about the place. We'd had half a day of frustration, long drives out and back, and the cooling touch of freshwater on my body, and the ocean-soaring bird, and the speed of those low-flying clouds, their massive tumbling summits, and my weightless drift, the slow turning in the pool, like some remote-controlled rapture, made me feel I knew what it was to be in the world. It was special, yes. The dream of Creation that glows at the edge of the serious traveler's search. Naked. It remained only for Jill to come walking through the sheer curtains and slip silently into the pool.

We had dinner in the pavilion, overlooking a quiet sea. The tables were only one-quarter occupied. The European woman, our taxi companion, sat in the far corner. I nodded. Either she didn't notice or chose not to acknowledge.

"Shouldn't we ask her to join us?"

"She doesn't want to," I said.

"We're Americans, after all. We're famous for asking people to join us."

"She chose the most remote table. She's happy there."

"She could be an economist from the Soviet bloc. What do you think? Or someone doing a health study for the U.N."

"Way off."

"A youngish widow, Swiss, here to forget."

"Not Swiss."

"German," she said.

"Yes."

"Wandering aimlessly through the islands. Sitting at the most remote tables."

"They weren't surprised when I said we wanted breakfast at four-thirty."

"The whole island has to adjust to that rotten stinking airline. It is awful, awful."

Jill wore a long tunic and gauze pants. We left our shoes

under the table and took a walk along the beach, wandering knee-high into the water at one point. A security guard stood under the palms, watching us. When we got back to the table, the waiter brought coffee.

"There's always the chance they'll be able to take two standbys but not three," Jill said. "I absolutely have to be back for Wednesday but I think we ought to stick together all the same."

"We're a team. We've been a team all through this thing."

"How many flights to Barbados tomorrow?"

"Only two. What happens Wednesday?"

"Bernie Gladman comes down from Buffalo."

"The earth is scorched for miles around."

"It took only six weeks to set up the meeting."

"We'll get out. If not at six forty-five, then late in the afternoon. Of course if that happens, we miss our connecting flight in Barbados."

"I don't want to hear," she said.

"Unless we go to Martinique instead."

"You're the only man who's ever understood that boredom and fear are one and the same to me."

"I try not to exploit this knowledge."

"You love to be boring. You seek out boring situations."

"Airports."

"Hour-long taxi rides," she said.

First the tops of the palms started bending. Then the rain hit, ringing down in heavy splashes on the stone path. When it let up, we walked across the lawn to our suite.

Watching Jill undress. Rum in a toothbrush glass. The sound and force of the wind. The skin near my eyes feeling cracked from ten days of sun and blowing weather.

I had trouble falling asleep. After the wind died, finally, the first thing I heard was roosters crowing, what seemed hundreds of them, off in the hills. Minutes later the dogs started barking.

We rode out in first light. Nine men with machetes walked single-file along the road.

We established that the other woman's name was Christa. She and Jill made small talk for the first few miles. Then Jill lowered her head toward the open book.

It rained once, briefly.

I'd expected half a dozen people to be in the terminal at that hour. It was jammed. They pushed toward the counter. It was hard to get around them because of luggage and boxes and birdcages and small children.

"This is crazy," Jill said. "Where are we? I don't believe this is happening."

"The plane will be empty when it gets here, or close to it. That's what I'm counting on. And many of these people are standbys. We're two and three, remember."

"God, if you exist, please get me off this island."

She was very near crying. I left her by the door and tried to get up to the edge of the counter. I heard the plane approach and touch down.

In minutes the regular passengers were nearly all cleared away from the counter and were forming a line across the room. The heat was already drenching. Among those of us who remained clustered, there were small gusts of desperation—a vehemence of motion, gesture and expression.

I heard the clerk call our names. I got to the counter and leaned way over. His head and mine were almost touching. One would go, I told him, and one would not. I gave him Jill's ticket. Then I hurried back to get her luggage and carry it to the small platform next to the counter. Her mouth gaped open and her arms shot out from her sides in a kind of silent-movie figure of surprise. She started after me with one of my own bags.

"You're going alone," I said. "You have to fill out a form at the booth. Where's your passport?"

Rid of the luggage, I walked her over to immigration and held one of her tote bags as she filled out the yellow form. Between lines, she kept looking at me anxiously. Confusion everywhere. The space around us glassy and bright.

"Here's money for the airport tax. They had room for only one of us. It's stupid for you not to go."

"But we agreed."

"It's stupid not to go."

"I don't like this."

"You'll be all right."

"What about you?"

"I'll marry a native woman and learn how to paint."

"We can charter. Let's try, even if it's just the two of us."

"It's hopeless. Nothing works here."

"I don't like leaving this way. This is so awful. I don't want to go."

"Darling Jill," I said.

I watched her walk toward the ramp at the tail section. Soon the props were turning. I went inside and saw Christa near the door. I got my bags and walked out to the road. Rupert was sitting on a bench outside the gift shop. I had to walk about ten yards down the road before I was able to catch his eye. I looked back at Christa. She picked up her suitcase. Then the three of us from our separate locations started toward the car.

I was beginning to learn when a certain set of houses would appear, where the worst turns were, when and on which side the terrain would fall away to a stretch of deep jungle. She sat next to me absently rubbing an insect bite on her left forearm.

We went to the same hotel and I asked for a pool suite. We followed a maid along the beach and then up the path to one of the garden gates. The way Christa reacted to the garden and pool, I realized she'd spent the previous night in one of the beach units, which were ordinary.

When we were alone, I followed her into the bathroom. She took some lotion out of her makeup kit and poured a small amount on a piece of cotton. Slowly she moved the cotton over her face.

"You were number seven," I said.

"They took four, only."

"You would have come back alone? Or stayed at the airport?"

"I have very little money. I didn't expect."

"They have no computer."

"I have gone out. I have called them from the hotel where I was. They have different lists. Two times they could not find my name anywhere. And there is no way to know when a flight is canceled."

"The plane doesn't come."

"This is true," she said. "The plane doesn't come and you know you have gone out for nothing."

I held her face in my hands.

"Is this nothing?"

"I don't know."

"You feel."

"Yes, I feel."

She walked inside and sat on the bed. Then she looked toward the doorway, taking me in—a delayed evaluation. After a period of what seemed dead silence, I was aware of the sound of waves rolling softly in, and realized I'd been hearing it all along, the ocean, the break and run of moving water. Christa kept her eyes on me as she reached back toward her handbag, which was sitting in the middle of the bed, and then as she felt inside for cigarettes.

"How much money do you have?" I said.

"One hundred dollars, E.C."

"Less than two trips out and back."

"It's amusing, yes. This is how we must count our money."

"Did you sleep last night?"

"No," she said.

"The wind was incredible. The wind kept blowing. It blew hard until dawn. I love the sound and feel of that kind of wind. It was warm, it was almost hot. It bent those trees out there. You could hear the rush it makes through the trees. That heavy rushing scatter-sound it makes."

"When you heard how loud it was and felt how hard it was blowing, you could not believe it would be warm."

When everything is new, the pleasures are skin-deep. I found it mysteriously satisfying to say her name aloud, to recite the colors of her body. Hair and eyes and hands. The new snow of her breasts. Absolutely nothing seemed trite. I wanted to make lists and classifications. Simple, basic, true. Her voice was soft and knowing. Her eyes were sad. Her left hand trembled at times. She was a woman who'd had troubles in her life, a hauntingly bad marriage, perhaps, or the death of a dear friend. Her mouth was sensual. She let her head ease back when she listened. The brown of her hair was ordinary, with traces of gray, short strokes or flashes that seemed to come and go in varying light.

All this I said to her, and more, describing in some detail exactly how she appeared to me, and Christa seemed pleased by these attentions.

We used the morning in bed. After lunch I floated in the pool. Christa lay naked in the shade, moving farther into it whenever the sun line reached her elbow or the edge of her pink heel.

"We must start thinking," she said. "There is the plane at five."

"We're not even wait-listed anymore. We left without telling them to move up our names. It's useless."

"I must get out."

"I'll call later. I'll give them our names. We'll see what the numbers are. We can leave tomorrow. Three flights tomorrow."

She draped herself in a large towel and sat on the steps that led to the patio. It was clear there was something she wanted to say. I stood at chest level in the water.

This was the fourth day she'd been trying to get off the island. She had begun to be deeply afraid these past twenty-four hours. The ordeals at the airport, she said, had made her feel helpless and pathetic and lost. The strange way they spoke. Her diminishing supply of money. The cab rides through the mountains. The rain and heat. And the edge, the dark edge, the inwrought mood or tone, the ominous logic of the place. It was all dreamlike, a nightmare of isolation and constraint. She had to get off the island. We would have these hours together. This episode, she called it. But then I must help her get out.

She looked solemn in her white towel. I bobbed several times in the water. Then I climbed out and went inside to call the airline. A man said he had no record of our names. I told him we had valid tickets and explained some of our difficulties. He said to come out at six in the morning. We would all know more.

We had dinner in the suite. With a pencil I sketched her face in profile on the back of a linen napkin. We took our dessert out to the garden. I sketched her again, full figure this time, on a piece of hotel stationery. The ocean. The coastal sweep.

"You paint, then?"

"I write."

"Yes, a writer?"

"What is it that smells so fantastic? Is that jasmine? I wish I knew the names."

"It's very pleasant, a garden."

"Aside from getting out, just getting off the island, do you have to be somewhere at a particular time?"

"I have to fly Barbados–London. There are people who are meeting me."

"People waiting."

"Yes."

"In an English garden."

"In two small rooms, with babies crying."

"You smile. She smiles."

"This is a tremendous thing."

"A secret smile, this smile of hers. Deep and private. But engaging all the same."

"No one has seen this in years. It hurts my face to do."

"Christa Landauer."

A man came with brandy. Christa sat in an old robe. The night was clear.

"You have a desire to go unnoticed," I said.

"How do you see this?"

"You want to be indistinct. I see this in different ways. Clothes, walk, posture. Your face, most of all. You had a different face not so long ago. I'm sure of that."

"What else do we know about each other?"

"What we can see."

"Touch. What we touch."

"Speak German," I said.

"Why?"

"I like hearing it."

"Do you know the language?"

"I want to hear the sound. I like the sound of it. It's full of heavy metal. I know how to say hello and goodbye."

"This is all?"

"Speak naturally. Say anything at all. Be conversational."

"We will be German in bed."

She sat with one leg up on a chair, out of the robe, and held her brandy glass and cigarette in the same hand.

"Are you listening?"

"To what?"

"Listen carefully."

"The waves," she said.

In a while we went inside. I watched her walk to the bed.

She moved a pillow out of the way and lay back on the bed, looking straight up, one arm hanging over the side. With her index finger she tapped cigarette ash onto the floor. Smoke climbed along her arm. Women in random positions, women lazing, have always aroused in me a powerful delight, women carelessly at rest, and I knew this image of Christa would become in time a recurring memory, her eyes open and very remote, the depths of stillness in her face, the shabby robe, the bed in disarray, the sense she conveyed of pensive reflection, of aloneness and somber distances, the smoke that rose along her arm, seeming to cling to it.

I called the desk. The man said he would have someone come with breakfast at four-thirty and would have Rupert sitting outside in his taxi at five.

The wind came up suddenly, rattling the louvres and blowing right through the room, papers sailing, the curtains lifted high. Christa put out her cigarette and turned off the light.

When I opened my eyes, much later, the desk lamp was on and she sat in a chair, in her robe, reading some papers. I tried reaching for my watch. The door and louvres were shut but I could hear rain falling.

"What time is it?"

"Go to sleep."

"Did we miss the call?"

"There's still time. They will ring the bell by the gate. An hour yet."

"I want you next to me."

"I must finish," she said. "Go to sleep."

I managed to prop myself on an elbow.

"What are you reading?"

"It's work. It's very dull. You don't want to know. We don't ask, you and I. You're half sleeping or you wouldn't ask."

"Will you come to bed soon?"

"Yes, soon."

"If I'm asleep, will you wake me?"

"Yes."

"Will you slide the door open a little, so we can feel the air?"

"Yes," she said. "Of course. Whatever you wish."

I lay back and closed my eyes. I thought of those sand islands out there, two days' sail, and surf flashing on the reefs, and the way the undersides of the gulls looked green from the bright water.

Again, again, the broad-leaved trees and tangled lowlands, the winding climb through smoke and rain. Some circumstance of light this particular morning gave the landscape a subtle coloration. Distances were not so vivid and living. There was only the one deep green, with elusive shadings. We were in the late stages now, about forty-five minutes out, and I was thinking it could still change, some rude blend of weather might yet transform the land, producing texture and dimension, leaps of green light, those waverings and rays, and the near consciousness we always seem to find in zones of overgrown terrain. Christa rubbed her neck, sleepily. I kept peering out and up. In the foreground, along the road, were women in faded skirts, appearing in twos and threes, periodically, women coming into the damp glow, faces strong-boned, some with baskets on their heads, looking in, shoulders back, their bare arms shining.

"This time we get out," Christa said.

"You feel lucky."

"We don't even wait. First flight."

"What if it doesn't happen?"

"Don't even whisper this."

"Will you go back with me?"

"I don't listen to this."

"It's crazy to stay," I said. "Seven- or eight-hour wait. We'll know our status. I'll check everything with the man. Rupert will wait for us. He'll take us back to the hotel. We'll have some time together. Then we'll come back out. We'll get the two o'clock flight, or the five, depending on our status. The important thing right now is to clarify our status."

Rupert listened to the radio, his shoulders leaning into a snug turn.

"Do you enjoy this so much?" she said. "Back and forth?"

"I like to float."

"This is not an answer."

"Really, I like to float. I try to do some floating every chance I get."

"You should go back. Float six weeks."

"Not alone," I said.

She had on the same gray dress she'd been wearing two days earlier, in the dirt road outside the terminal, when I'd turned to see her standing politely to one side, her face contorted by the strong glare.

"How much longer? I know this place."

"Minutes," I said.

"This is where we nearly went off the road, the first time out, when smoke came pouring out of the front. I should have known then. It would be disaster to the end."

"Rupert wouldn't let that happen, Rupert, would you?"

"Watching the whole car disappear in smoke," she said.

I looked over at her and we both smiled. Rupert tapped the steering wheel in time to the music. We passed some houses and climbed the final grade.

I took Christa's ticket and asked her to wait in the taxi. The luggage would also stay until we were sure we'd be able to board. Several people mingled outside the terminal. A heavyset man, Indian or Pakistani, stood by the door. I'd seen him near the counter the day before, hemmed in, sweating, in a striped blazer. Something about him now, an attitude of introspection, his almost eerie calm, made me feel I ought to stop alongside.

"There is a rumor it went down," he said.

We didn't look at each other.

"How many aboard?"

"Eight passenger, three crew."

I went inside. There were only two people in the terminal and the counter was empty. I went behind the counter and opened the office door. Two men in white shirts sat facing each other across desks arranged back to back.

"Is it true?" I said. "It went down?"

They looked at me.

"The flight from Trinidad. The six forty-five. To Barbados. It's not down?"

"Flight is canceled," one of them said.

"Outside they're saying it crashed in the goddamn ocean."

"No, no—canceled."

"What happened?"

"No opportunity to take off."

"Winds," the second one said.

"They had a whole ray of problems."

21

"So it was only canceled," I said, "and there's nothing major."

"You didn't call. You have to call before coming out. Always call."

"Other people call," the second one said. "That's why you're coming all alone."

I showed them the tickets and one of them wrote down our names and said he expected the plane to be here in time for the two o'clock departure.

"What's our status?" I said.

He told me to call before coming out. I walked through the terminal, now deserted. The stocky man was still outside the door.

"It's not down," I told him.

He looked at me, thinking.

"Is it up, then?"

I shook my head.

"Winds," I said.

Some kids ran by. Rupert's cab was parked in a small open area about thirty yards away. There was no one at the wheel. When I got closer I saw Christa lean forward in the backseat. She spotted me and got out, waiting by the open door.

It would be best to start with the rumor of a crash. She would be relieved to hear it wasn't true. This would make it easier for her to accept the cancellation.

But when I started talking I realized tactics were pointless. Her face went slowly dead. All the selves collapsing inward. She was inaccessible and utterly still. I kept on explaining, not knowing what else to do, aware that I was speaking even more clearly than one usually does to foreigners. It rained a little. I tried to explain that we'd most likely get out later in the day. I spoke slowly and distinctly. The children came running.

Christa's lips moved, although she didn't say anything. She pushed by me and walked quickly down the road. She was in the underbrush behind a tarpaper shack when I caught up to her. She fell into me, trembling.

"It's all right," I said. "You're not alone, no harm will come, it's just one day. It's all right, it's all right. We'll just be together, that's all. One more day, that's all."

I held her from behind, speaking very softly, my mouth touching the curve of her right ear.

"We'll be alone in the hotel. Almost the only guests. You can rest all day and think of nothing, nothing. It doesn't matter who you are or how you got stuck here or where you're going next. You don't even have to move. You lie in the shade. I know you like to lie in the shade."

I touched her face gently with the back of my hand, caressing again and again, that lovely word.

"We'll just be together. You can rest and sleep, and tonight we'll have a quiet brandy, and you'll feel better about things. I know you will, I'm sure of it, I'm absolutely convinced. You're not alone. It's all right, it's all right. We'll have these final hours, that's all. And you'll speak to me in German."

In a light rain we walked back along the road toward the open door of the taxi. Rupert was at the wheel, wearing his silver medal. He had the motor running.

HUMAN MOMENTS
IN WORLD WAR III

A note about Vollmer. He no longer describes the earth as a library globe or a map that has come alive, as a cosmic eye staring into deep space. This last was his most ambitious fling at imagery. The war has changed the way he sees the earth. The earth is land and water, the dwelling place of mortal men, in elevated dictionary terms. He doesn't see it anymore (storm-spiraled, sea-bright, breathing heat and haze and color) as an occasion for picturesque language, for easeful play or speculation.

At two hundred and twenty kilometers we see ship wakes and the larger airports. Icebergs, lightning bolts, sand dunes. I point out lava flows and cold-core eddies. That silver ribbon off the Irish coast, I tell him, is an oil slick.

This is my third orbital mission, Vollmer's first. He is an engineering genius, a communications and weapons genius, and maybe other kinds of genius as well. As mission specialist I'm content to be in charge. (The word *specialist*, in the standard usage of Colorado Command, refers here to someone who does not specialize.) Our spacecraft is designed primarily to gather intelligence. The refinement of the quantum-burn technique enables us to make frequent adjustments of orbit without firing rockets every time. We swing out into high wide trajectories, the whole earth as our psychic light, to inspect unmanned and possibly hostile satellites. We orbit tightly, snugly, take intimate looks at surface activities in untraveled places.

The banning of nuclear weapons has made the world safe for war.

I try not to think big thoughts or submit to rambling abstractions. But the urge sometimes comes over me. Earth orbit puts men into philosophical temper. How can we help it? We see the planet complete, we have a privileged vista. In our attempts to be equal to the experience, we tend to meditate importantly on subjects like the human condition. It makes a man feel *universal*, floating over the continents, seeing the rim of the world, a line as clear as a compass arc, knowing it is just a turning of the bend to Atlantic twilight, to sediment plumes and kelp beds, an island chain glowing in the dusky sea.

I tell myself it is only scenery. I want to think of our life here as ordinary, as a housekeeping arrangement, an unlikely but workable setup caused by a housing shortage or spring floods in the valley.

Vollmer does the systems checklist and goes to his hammock to rest. He is twenty-three years old, a boy with a longish head and close-cropped hair. He talks about northern Minnesota as he removes the objects in his personal-preference kit, placing them on an adjacent Velcro surface for tender inspection. I have a 1901 silver dollar in my personal-preference kit. Little else of note. Vollmer has graduation pictures, bottle caps, small stones from his backyard. I don't know whether he chose these items himself or whether they were pressed on him by parents who feared that his life in space would be lacking in human moments.

Our hammocks are human moments, I suppose, although I don't know whether Colorado Command planned it that way. We eat hot dogs and almond crunch bars and apply lip balm as part of the presleep checklist. We wear slippers at the firing panel. Vollmer's football jersey is a human moment. Outsize, purple and white, of polyester mesh, bearing the number 79, a big man's number, a prime of no particular distinction, it makes him look stoop-shouldered, abnormally long-framed.

"I still get depressed on Sundays," he says.

"Do we have Sundays here?"

"No, but they have them there and I still feel them. I always know when it's Sunday."

"Why do you get depressed?"

"The slowness of Sundays. Something about the glare, the smell of warm grass, the church service, the relatives visiting in nice clothes. The whole day kind of lasts forever."

"I didn't like Sundays either."

"They were slow but not lazy-slow. They were long and hot, or long and cold. In summer my grandmother made lemonade. There was a routine. The whole day was kind of set up beforehand and the routine almost never changed. Orbital routine is different. It's satisfying. It gives our time a shape and substance. Those Sundays were shapeless despite the fact you knew what was coming, who was coming, what we'd all say. You knew the first words out of the mouth of each person before anyone spoke. I was the only kid in the group. People were happy to see me. I used to want to hide."

"What's wrong with lemonade?" I ask.

A battle-management satellite, unmanned, reports high-energy laser activity in orbital sector Dolores. We take out our laser kits and study them for half an hour. The beaming procedure is complex, and because the panel operates on joint control only, we must rehearse the sets of established measures with the utmost care.

A note about the earth. The earth is the preserve of day and night. It contains a sane and balanced variation, a natural waking and sleeping, or so it seems to someone deprived of this tidal effect.

This is why Vollmer's remark about Sundays in Minnesota struck me as interesting. He still feels, or claims he feels, or thinks he feels, that inherently earthbound rhythm.

To men at this remove, it is as though things exist in their particular physical form in order to reveal the hidden simplicity of some powerful mathematical truth. The earth reveals to us the simple awesome beauty of day and night. It is there to contain and incorporate these conceptual events.

Vollmer in his shorts and suction clogs resembles a high school swimmer, all but hairless, an unfinished man not aware he is open to cruel scrutiny, not aware he is without devices, standing with arms folded in a place of echoing voices and chlorine fumes. There is something stupid in the sound of his voice. It is too direct, a deep voice from high in the mouth, slightly insistent, a little loud. Vollmer has never said a stupid thing in my presence. It is just his voice that is stupid, a grave and naked bass, a voice without inflection or breath.

We are not cramped here. The flight deck and crew quarters are thoughtfully designed. Food is fair to good. There are books, videocassettes, news and music. We do the manual checklists, the oral checklists, the simulated firings with no sign of boredom or carelessness. If anything, we are getting better at our tasks all the time. The only danger is conversation.

I try to keep our conversations on an everyday plane. I make it a point to talk about small things, routine things. This makes sense to me. It seems a sound tactic, under the circumstances, to restrict our talk to familiar topics, minor matters. I want to build a structure of the commonplace. But Vollmer has a tendency to bring up enormous subjects. He wants to talk about war and the weapons of war. He wants to discuss global strategies, global aggressions. I tell him now that he has stopped describing the earth as a cosmic eye he wants to see it as a game board or computer model. He looks at me plain-faced and tries to get me into a theoretical argument: selective space-based attacks versus long, drawn-out, well-modulated land-sea-air engagements. He quotes experts, mentions sources. What am I supposed to say? He will suggest that people are disappointed in the war. The war is dragging into its third week. There is a sense in which it is worn out, played out. He gathers this from the news broadcasts we periodically receive. Something in the announcer's voice hints at a letdown, a fatigue, a faint bitterness about—*something*. Vollmer is probably right about this. I've heard it myself in the tone of the broadcaster's voice, in the voice of Colorado Command, despite the fact that our news is censored, that they are not telling us things they feel we shouldn't know, in our special situation, our exposed and sensitive position. In his direct and stupid-sounding and uncannily perceptive way, young Vollmer says that people are not enjoying this war to the same extent that people have always enjoyed and nourished themselves on war, as a heightening, a periodic intensity. What I object to in Vollmer is that he often shares my deep-reaching and most reluctantly held convictions. Coming from that mild face, in that earnest resonant run-on voice, these ideas unnerve and worry me as they never do when they remain unspoken. I want words to be secretive, to cling to a darkness in the deepest interior. Vollmer's candor exposes something painful.

It is not too early in the war to discern nostalgic references to earlier wars. All wars refer back. Ships, planes, entire operations are named after ancient battles, simpler weapons, what we perceive as conflicts of nobler intent. This recon-interceptor is called *Tomahawk II*. When I sit at the firing panel I look at a photograph of Vollmer's granddad when he was a young man in sagging khakis and a shallow helmet, standing in a bare field, a rifle strapped to his shoulder. This is a human moment, and it reminds me that war, among other things, is a form of longing.

We dock with the command station, take on food, exchange cassettes. The war is going well, they tell us, although it isn't likely they know much more than we do.

Then we separate.

The maneuver is flawless and I am feeling happy and satisfied, having resumed human contact with the nearest form of the outside world, having traded quips and manly insults, traded voices, traded news and rumors—buzzes, rumbles, scuttlebutt. We stow our supplies of broccoli and apple cider and fruit cocktail and butterscotch pudding. I feel a homey emotion, putting away the colorfully packaged goods, a sensation of prosperous well-being, the consumer's solid comfort.

Vollmer's T-shirt bears the word INSCRIPTION.

"People had hoped to be caught up in something bigger than themselves," he says. "They thought it would be a shared crisis. They would feel a sense of shared purpose, shared destiny. Like a snowstorm that blankets a large city — but lasting months, lasting years, carrying everyone along, creating fellow feeling where there was only suspicion and fear. Strangers talking to each other, meals by candlelight when the power fails. The war would ennoble everything we say and do. What was impersonal would become personal. What was solitary would be shared. But what happens when the sense of shared crisis begins to dwindle much sooner than anyone expected? We begin to think the feeling lasts longer in snowstorms."

A note about selective noise. Forty-eight hours ago I was monitoring data on the mission console when a voice broke in on my report to Colorado Command. The voice was unenhanced, heavy with static. I checked my headset, checked the switches and lights. Seconds later the command signal resumed and I heard our flight-dynamics officer ask me to switch to the redundant sense frequencer. I did this but it only caused the weak voice to return, a voice that carried with it a strange and unspecifiable poignancy. I seemed somehow to recognize it. I don't mean I knew who was speaking. It was the tone I recognized, the touching quality of some half-remembered and tender event, even through the static, the sonic mist.

In any case, Colorado Command resumed transmission in a matter of seconds.

"We have a deviate, Tomahawk."

"We copy. There's a voice."

"We have gross oscillation here."

"There's some interference. I have gone redundant but I'm not sure it's helping."

"We are clearing an outframe to locate source."

"Thank you, Colorado."

"It is probably just selective noise. You are negative red on the step-function quad."

"It was a voice," I told them.

"We have just received an affirm on selective noise."

"I could hear words, in English."

"We copy selective noise."

"Someone was talking, Colorado."

"What do you think selective noise is?"

"I don't know what it is."

"You are getting a spill from one of the unmanneds."

"If it's an unmanned, how could it be sending a voice?"

"It is not a voice as such, Tomahawk. It is selective noise. We have some real firm telemetry on that."

"It sounded like a voice."

"It is supposed to sound like a voice. But it is not a voice as such. It is enhanced."

"It sounded unenhanced. It sounded human in all sorts of ways."

"It is signals and they are spilling from geosynchronous

orbit. This is your deviate. You are getting voice codes from twenty-two thousand miles. It is basically a weather report. We will correct, Tomahawk. In the meantime, advise you stay redundant."

About ten hours later Vollmer heard the voice. Then he heard two or three other voices. They were people speaking, people in conversation. He gestured to me as he listened, pointed to the headset, then raised his shoulders, held his hands apart to indicate surprise and bafflement. In the swarming noise (as he said later) it wasn't easy to get the drift of what people were saying. The static was frequent, the references were somewhat elusive, but Vollmer mentioned how intensely affecting these voices were, even when the signals were at their weakest. One thing he did know: it wasn't selective noise. A quality of purest, sweetest sadness issued from remote space. He wasn't sure, but he thought there was also a background noise integral to the conversation. Laughter. The sound of people laughing.

In other transmissions we've been able to recognize theme music, an announcer's introduction, wisecracks and bursts of applause, commercials for products whose long-lost brand names evoke the golden antiquity of great cities buried in sand and river silt.

Somehow we are picking up signals from radio programs of forty, fifty, sixty years ago.

Our current task is to collect imagery data on troop deployment. Vollmer surrounds his Hasselblad, engrossed in some microadjustment. There is a seaward bulge of stratocumulus. Sun glint and littoral drift. I see blooms of plankton in a blue of such Persian richness it seems an animal rapture, a color change to express some form of intuitive delight. As the surface features unfurl I list them aloud by name. It is the only game I play in space, reciting the earth names, the nomenclature of contour and structure. Glacial scour, moraine debris. Shatter-coning at the edge of a multi-ring impact site. A resurgent caldera, a mass of castellated rimrock. Over the sand seas now. Parabolic dunes, star dunes, straight dunes with radial crests. The emptier the land, the more luminous and precise the names for its features. Vollmer says the thing science does best is name the features of the world.

He has degrees in science and technology. He was a scholarship winner, an honors student, a research assistant. He ran science projects, read technical papers in the deep-pitched earnest voice that rolls off the roof of his mouth. As mission specialist (generalist), I sometimes resent his non-scientific perceptions, the glimmerings of maturity and balanced judgment. I am beginning to feel slightly preempted. I want him to stick to systems, onboard guidance, data parameters. His human insights make me nervous.

"I'm happy," he says.

These words are delivered with matter-of-fact finality, and the simple statement affects me powerfully. It frightens me, in fact. What does he mean he's happy? Isn't happiness totally outside our frame of reference? How can he think it is possible to be happy here? I want to say to him, "This is just a housekeeping arrangement, a series of more or less routine tasks. Attend to your tasks, do your testing, run through your checklists." I want to say, "Forget the measure of our vision, the sweep of things, the war itself, the terrible death. Forget the overarching night, the stars as static points, as math-

34

ematical fields. Forget the cosmic solitude, the upwelling awe and dread."

I want to say, "Happiness is not a fact of this experience, at least not to the extent that one is bold enough to speak of it."

Laser technology contains a core of foreboding and myth. It is a clean sort of lethal package we are dealing with, a well-behaved beam of photons, an engineered coherence, but we approach the weapon with our minds full of ancient warnings and fears. (There ought to be a term for this ironic condition: primitive fear of the weapons we are advanced enough to design and produce.) Maybe this is why the project managers were ordered to work out a firing procedure that depends on the coordinated actions of two men—two temperaments, two souls—operating the controls together. Fear of the power of light, the pure stuff of the universe.

A single dark mind in a moment of inspiration might think it liberating to fling a concentrated beam at some lumbering humpbacked Boeing making its commercial rounds at thirty thousand feet.

Vollmer and I approach the firing panel. The panel is designed in such a way that the joint operators must sit back to back. The reason for this, although Colorado Command never specifically said so, is to keep us from seeing each other's face. Colorado wants to be sure that weapons personnel in particular are not influenced by each other's tics and perturbations. We are back to back, therefore, harnessed in our seats, ready to begin, Vollmer in his purple-and-white jersey, his fleeced pad-abouts.

This is only a test.

I start the playback. At the sound of a prerecorded voice

command, we each insert a modal key in its proper slot. Together we count down from five and then turn the keys one-quarter left. This puts the system in what is called an open-minded mode. We count down from three. The enhanced voice says, *You are open-minded now.*

Vollmer speaks into his voiceprint analyzer.

"This is code B for *bluegrass.* Request voice-identity clearance."

We count down from five and then speak into our voiceprint analyzers. We say whatever comes into our heads. The point is simply to produce a voiceprint that matches the print in the memory bank. This ensures that the men at the panel are the same men authorized to be there when the system is in an open-minded mode.

This is what comes into my head: "I am standing at the corner of Fourth and Main, where thousands are dead of unknown causes, their scorched bodies piled in the street."

We count down from three. The enhanced voice says, *You are cleared to proceed to lock-in position.*

We turn our modal keys half right. I activate the logic chip and study the numbers on my screen. Vollmer disengages voiceprint and puts us in voice circuit rapport with the onboard computer's sensing mesh. We count down from five. The enhanced voice says, *You are locked in now.*

As we move from one step to the next a growing satisfaction passes through me—the pleasure of elite and secret skills, a life in which every breath is governed by specific rules, by patterns, codes, controls. I try to keep the results of the operation out of my mind, the whole point of it, the outcome of these sequences of precise and esoteric steps. But often I fail. I let the image in, I think the thought, I even say the word at times. This is confusing, of course. I feel tricked. My pleasure feels betrayed, as if it had a life of its own, a childlike or intelligent-animal existence independent of the man at the firing panel.

We count down from five. Vollmer releases the lever that unwinds the systems-purging disk. My pulse marker shows green at three-second intervals. We count down from three. We turn the modal keys three-quarters right. I activate the beam sequencer. We turn the keys one-quarter right. We count down from three. Bluegrass music plays over the squawk box. The enhanced voice says, *You are moded to fire now.*

We study our world-map kits.

"Don't you sometimes feel a power in you?" Vollmer says. "An extreme state of good health, sort of. An *arrogant* healthiness. That's it. You are feeling so good you begin thinking you're a little superior to other people. A kind of life-strength. An optimism about yourself that you generate almost at the expense of others. Don't you sometimes feel this?"

(Yes, as a matter of fact.)

"There's probably a German word for it. But the point I want to make is that this powerful feeling is so—I don't know—*delicate*. That's it. One day you feel it, the next day you are suddenly puny and doomed. A single little thing goes wrong, you feel doomed, you feel utterly weak and defeated and unable to act powerfully or even sensibly. Everyone else is lucky, you are unlucky, hapless, sad, ineffectual and doomed."

(Yes, yes.)

By chance, we are over the Missouri River now, looking toward the Red Lakes of Minnesota. I watch Vollmer go through his map kit, trying to match the two worlds. This is a deep and mysterious happiness, to confirm the accuracy of a map. He seems immensely satisfied. He keeps saying, *"That's it, that's it."*

Vollmer talks about childhood. In orbit he has begun to think about his early years for the first time. He is surprised at the power of these memories. As he speaks he keeps his head turned to the window. Minnesota is a human moment. Upper Red Lake, Lower Red Lake. He clearly feels he can see himself there.

"Kids don't take walks," he says. "They don't sunbathe or sit on the porch."

He seems to be saying that children's lives are too well supplied to accommodate the spells of reinforced being that the rest of us depend on. A deft enough thought but not to be pursued. It is time to prepare for a quantum burn.

We listen to the old radio shows. Light flares and spreads across the blue-banded edge, sunrise, sunset, the urban grids in shadow. A man and a woman trade well-timed remarks, light, pointed, bantering. There is a sweetness in the tenor voice of the young man singing, a simple vigor that time and distance and random noise have enveloped in eloquence and yearning. Every sound, every lilt of strings has this veneer of age. Vollmer says he remembers these programs, although of course he has never heard them before. What odd happenstance, what flourish or grace of the laws of physics enables us to pick up these signals? Traveled voices, chambered and dense. At times they have the detached and surreal quality of aural hallucination, voices in attic rooms, the complaints of dead relatives. But the sound effects are full of urgency and verve. Cars turn dangerous corners, crisp gunfire fills the night. It was, it is, wartime. Wartime for Duz and Grape-Nuts Flakes. Comedians make fun of the way the enemy talks. We hear hysterical mock German, moonshine Japanese. The cities are in light, the listening millions, fed, met comfortably in drowsy rooms, at war, as the night comes softly down. Vollmer says he recalls specific moments, the comic inflections, the announcer's fat-man laughter. He recalls individual voices rising from the laughter of the studio audience, the cackle of a St. Louis businessman, the brassy wail of a high-shouldered blonde just arrived in California, where women wear their hair this year in aromatic bales.

Vollmer drifts across the wardroom upside down, eating an almond crunch.

He sometimes floats free of his hammock, sleeping in a fetal crouch, bumping into walls, adhering to a corner of the ceiling grid.

"Give me a minute to think of the name," he says in his sleep.

He says he dreams of vertical spaces from which he looks, as a boy, at—*something*. My dreams are the heavy kind, the kind that are hard to wake from, to rise out of. They are strong enough to pull me back down, dense enough to leave me with a heavy head, a drugged and bloated feeling. There are episodes of faceless gratification, vaguely disturbing.

"It's almost unbelievable when you think of it, how they live there in all that ice and sand and mountainous wilderness. Look at it," he says. "Huge barren deserts, huge oceans. How do they endure all those terrible things? The floods

DON DeLILLO

alone. The earthquakes alone make it crazy to live there.
Look at those fault systems. They're so big, there's so many
of them. The volcanic eruptions alone. What could be more
frightening than a volcanic eruption? How do they endure
avalanches, year after year, with numbing regularity? It's
hard to believe people live there. The floods alone. You can
see whole huge discolored areas, all flooded out, washed
out. How do they survive, where do they go? Look at the
cloud buildups. Look at that swirling storm center. What
about the people who live in the path of a storm like that?
It must be packing incredible winds. The lightning alone.
People exposed on beaches, near trees and telephone poles.
Look at the cities with their spangled lights spreading in all
directions. Try to imagine the crime and violence. Look at
the smoke pall hanging low. What does that mean in terms
of respiratory disorders? It's crazy. Who would live there?
The deserts, how they encroach. Every year they claim more
and more arable land. How enormous those snowfields are.
Look at the massive storm fronts over the ocean. There are
ships down there, small craft, some of them. Try to imagine
the waves, the rocking. The hurricanes alone. The tidal
waves. Look at those coastal communities exposed to tidal
waves. What could be more frightening than a tidal wave?
But they live there, they stay there. Where could they go?"

I want to talk to him about calorie intake, the effectiveness
of the earplugs and nasal decongestants. The earplugs are
human moments. The apple cider and the broccoli are
human moments. Vollmer himself is a human moment,
never more so than when he forgets there is a war.

The close-cropped hair and longish head. The mild blue

40

eyes that bulge slightly. The protuberant eyes of long-bodied people with stooped shoulders. The long hands and wrists. The mild face. The easy face of a handyman in a panel truck that has an extension ladder fixed to the roof and a scuffed license plate, green and white, with the state motto beneath the digits. That kind of face.

He offers to give me a haircut. What an interesting thing a haircut is, when you think of it. Before the war there were time slots reserved for such activities. Houston not only had everything scheduled well in advance but constantly monitored us for whatever meager feedback might result. We were wired, taped, scanned, diagnosed and metered. We were men in space, objects worthy of the most scrupulous care, the deepest sentiments and anxieties.

Now there is a war. Nobody cares about my hair, what I eat, how I feel about the spacecraft's decor, and it is not Houston but Colorado we are in touch with. We are no longer delicate biological specimens adrift in an alien environment. The enemy can kill us with its photons, its mesons, its charged particles faster than any calcium deficiency or trouble of the inner ear, faster than any dusting of micrometeoroids. The emotions have changed. We've stopped being candidates for an embarrassing demise, the kind of mistake or unforeseen event that tends to make a nation grope for the appropriate response. As men in war, we can be certain, dying, that we will arouse uncomplicated sorrows, the open and dependable feelings that grateful nations count on to embellish the simplest ceremony.

A note about the universe. Vollmer is on the verge of deciding that our planet is alone in harboring intelligent life. We are an accident and we happened only once. (What a remark to make, in egg-shaped orbit, to someone who doesn't want to discuss the larger questions.) He feels this way because of the war.

The war, he says, will bring about an end to the idea that the universe swarms, as they say, with life. Other astronauts have looked past the star points and imagined infinite possibility, grape-clustered worlds teeming with higher forms. But this was before the war. Our view is changing even now, his and mine, he says, as we drift across the firmament.

Is Vollmer saying that cosmic optimism is a luxury reserved for periods between world wars? Do we project our current failure and despair out toward the star clouds, the endless night? After all, he says, where are they? If they exist, why has there been no sign, not one, not any, not a single indication that serious people might cling to, not a whisper, a radio pulse, a shadow? The war tells us it is foolish to believe.

Our dialogues with Colorado Command are beginning to sound like computer-generated teatime chat. Vollmer tolerates Colorado's jargon only to a point. He is critical of their more debased locutions and doesn't mind letting them know. Why, then, if I agree with his views on this matter, am I becoming irritated by his complaints? Is he too young to champion the language? Does he have the experience, the professional standing to scold our flight-dynamics officer, our conceptual-paradigm officer, our status consultants on waste-management systems and evasion-related zonal options? Or is it something else completely, something unrelated to Colorado Command and our communications with them? Is it the sound of his voice? Is it just his *voice* that is driving me crazy?

*　*　*

Vollmer has entered a strange phase. He spends all his time at the window now, looking down at the earth. He says little or nothing. He simply wants to look, do nothing but look. The oceans, the continents, the archipelagoes. We are configured in what is called a cross-orbit series and there is no repetition from one swing around the earth to the next. He sits there looking. He takes meals at the window, does checklists at the window, barely glancing at the instruction sheets as we pass over tropical storms, over grass fires and major ranges. I keep waiting for him to return to his prewar habit of using quaint phrases to describe the earth: it's a beach ball, a sun-ripened fruit. But he simply looks out the window, eating almond crunches, the wrappers floating away. The view clearly fills his consciousness. It is powerful enough to silence him, to still the voice that rolls off the roof of his mouth, to leave him turned in the seat, twisted uncomfortably for hours at a time.

The view is endlessly fulfilling. It is like the answer to a lifetime of questions and vague cravings. It satisfies every childlike curiosity, every muted desire, whatever there is in him of the scientist, the poet, the primitive seer, the watcher of fire and shooting stars, whatever obsessions eat at the night side of his mind, whatever sweet and dreamy yearning he has ever felt for nameless places faraway, whatever earth sense he possesses, the neural pulse of some wilder awareness, a sympathy for beasts, whatever belief in an immanent vital force, the Lord of Creation, whatever secret harboring of the idea of human oneness, whatever wishfulness and simplehearted hope, whatever of too much and not enough, all at once and little by little, whatever burning urge to escape responsibility and routine, escape his own overspecialization, the circumscribed and inward-spiraling self, whatever remnants of his boyish longing to fly, his dreams of strange spaces and eerie heights, his fantasies of happy death, whatever indolent and sybaritic leanings—lotus-eater, smoker of grasses and herbs, blue-eyed gazer into space—all these are satisfied, all collected and massed in that living body, the sight he sees from the window.

"It is just so interesting," he says at last. "The colors and all."

The colors and all.

PART TWO

THE RUNNER

The runner took the turn slowly, watching ducks collect near the footbridge where a girl was scattering bread. The path roughly followed the outline of the pond, meandering through stands of trees. The runner listened to his even breathing. He was young and knew he could go harder but didn't want to spoil the sense of easy effort in the dying light, all the day's voices and noises drained out in steady sweat.

Traffic skimmed past. The girl took bread in fragments from her father and pitched them over the rail, holding her hand open like someone signaling five. The runner eased across the bridge. There were two women thirty yards ahead, walking along a path that led out to the street. A pigeon quick-stepped across the grass when the runner approached, leaning into his turn. The sun was in the trees beyond the parkway.

He was a quarter of the way down the path at the west side of the pond when a car came off the road, bouncing onto the sloped lawn. A breeze stirred up and the runner lifted his arms out, feeling the air slip into his T-shirt. A man got out of the car, moving fast. The runner passed an old couple on a bench. They were putting together sections of the newspaper, getting ready to leave. Purple loosestrife was coming into bloom along the near bank. He thought he would do four more laps, close to the edge of his endurance. There was a disturbance back there, over his right shoulder, a jump to another level. He looked back as he ran, seeing the old couple rise from the bench, unaware, and then the car on the grass, out of place, and a woman standing on a blanket looking toward the car, her hands raised, framing her face. He turned forward and ran past the sign that said the park closes at sundown, although there were no gates, no effective way to keep people out. The closing was strictly in the mind.

The car was old and bruised, the right rear fender painted a rustproof copper, and he heard staccato bursts from the exhaust pipe when it drove off.

He rounded the south end, watching two boys on bikes to see if something in their faces might hint at what was happening. They went past him, one to either side, and music leaked from the headset one of them wore. He saw the girl and her father at the end of the footbridge. A line of brushed light passed across the water. He saw the woman on the slope turned the other way now, looking down the parkway, and there were three or four people looking in the same direction, others with dogs just walking. He saw cars streaming past in the northbound lanes.

The woman was a short broad figure stuck to the blanket. She turned to some people moving toward her and began to call to them, not understanding that they knew she was in distress. They were around the blanket now and the runner watched them gesture for calm. Her voice was harsh and thick, with the breathless stammer of damaged speech. He couldn't tell what she was saying.

At the foot of a mild rise the path was soft and moist. The father looked toward the slope, a hand extended in front of him, palm up, and the girl selected bits of bread and turned toward the rail. Her face went tight in preparation. The runner approached the bridge. One of the men near the blanket came down to the path and jogged off toward the steps that led up to the street. He held his hand to his pocket to keep something from flying out. The girl wanted her father to watch her throw the bread.

Ten strides beyond the bridge the runner saw a woman coming toward him at an angle. She tilted her head in the hopeful way of a tourist who wishes to ask directions. He stopped but not completely, turning gradually so that they continued to face each other while he moved slowly backward on the path, legs still going in a runner's pump.

She said pleasantly, "Did you see what happened?"

"No. Just the car really. About two seconds."

"I saw the man."

"What happened?"

"I was leaving with my friend who lives just across the street here. We heard the car when it came over the curb. More or less bang on the grass. The father gets out and takes the little boy. No one had time to react. They get in the car and they're gone. I just said, 'Evelyn.' She went right off to telephone."

He was running in place now and she moved closer, a middle-aged woman with an inadvertent smile.

"I recognized you from the elevator," she said.

"How do you know it was his father?"

"It's all around us, isn't it? They have babies before they're ready. They don't know what they're getting into. It's one problem after another. Then they split up or the father gets in trouble with the police. Don't we see it all the time? He's unemployed, he uses drugs. One day he decides he's entitled to see more of his child. He wants to share custody. He broods for days. Then he comes around and they argue and he breaks up the furniture. The mother gets a court order. He has to stay away from the child."

They looked toward the slope, where the woman stood gesturing on the blanket. Another woman held some of her things, a sweater, a large cloth bag. A dog went bounding after seagulls down near the path and they lifted and settled again nearby.

"Look how heavy she is. We see more and more of this. Young women. They can't help it. It's a condition they're disposed to. How long are you in the building?"

"Four months."

"There are cases they walk in and start shooting. Common-law husbands. You can't separate a parent and expect everything works out. It's hard enough raising a child if you have the resources."

"But you can't be sure, can you?"

"I saw them both and I saw the child."

"Did she say anything?"

"She didn't have a chance. He grabbed the boy and got back in the car. I think she was totally frozen."

"Was anyone else in the car?"

"No. He dropped the boy on the seat and they were gone. I saw the whole thing. He wanted to share custody and the mother refused."

She was insistent, wincing in the light, and the runner remembered seeing her once in the laundry room, folding clothes with the same dazzled look.

"All right, we're looking at a woman in a terrible stricken

state," he said. "But I don't see a common-law husband, I don't see a separation, and I don't see a court order."

"How old are you?" she said.

"Twenty-three."

"Then you don't know."

He was surprised by the sharpness in her voice. He ran in place, unprepared and dripping, feeling heat rise from his chest. A police car swung up over the curbstone and everyone at the blanket turned and looked. The woman came near collapse when the policeman got out of the car. He moved in a practiced amble toward the group. She seemed to want to drop, to sink into the blanket and disappear. A sound came out of her, a desolation, and everyone moved a little closer, hands extended.

The runner used the moment to break off the dialogue. He went back to his laps, trying to recover the rhyme of stride and respiration. A work train passed beyond the trees on the other side of the pond, grave horn braying. He made the wide turn at the south end, feeling uneasy. He saw the small girl trail her father along a narrow path that led to an exit. He saw a second police car on the grass far to his left. The group was breaking up. He crossed the bridge, trying to spot the woman he'd been talking to. Ducks sailed in wobbly lines to the scattered bread.

Two more laps and he could call it quits.

He ran faster, still working at a cadence. The first police car left with the woman. He saw that the far end was empty now, sliding into deep shade. He made the turn, knowing he'd been wrong to cut the conversation so abruptly, even if she'd spoken sharply to him. A traffic cone jutted from the shallows. The runner approached the bridge.

Several strides into the last lap he veered onto the slope, gradually slowing to a walk. A policeman leaned on the door of the cruiser, talking to the last witness, a man who stood with his back to the runner. Cars hurried past, some with headlights shining. The policeman looked up from his notebook when the runner drew near.

"Sorry to interrupt, officer. I just wonder what the woman said. Was it her husband, someone she knew, who snatched the child?"

"What did you see?"

"Just the car. Blue with one discolored fender. Four-door. I didn't see the plates or notice the make. The slightest glimpse of the man, moving kind of crouched."

The policeman went back to his notes.

"It was a stranger," he said. "That's all she could tell us."

The other man, the witness, had half turned, and now the three of them stood in a loose circle, uncomfortably caught, eyes not meeting. The runner felt he'd entered a rivalry of delicate dimensions. He nodded at no one in particular and went back to the path. He started running again, going in a kind of skelter, elbows beating. A cluster of gulls sat motionless on the water.

The runner approached the end of the run. He stopped and leaned over deeply, hands on hips. After a moment he started walking along the path. The police car was gone and tire marks cut across the grass, three sets of curves that left ridges of thick dirt. He went out to the street and walked across the overpass toward a row of lighted shops. He never should have challenged her, no matter how neat and unyielding her version was. She'd only wanted to protect them both. What would you rather believe, a father who comes to take

52

his own child or someone lurching out of nowhere, out of dreaming space? He looked for her on the benches outside their building, where people often sat on warm evenings. She'd tried to extend the event in time, make it recognizable. Would you rather believe in a random shape, a man outside imagining? He saw her sitting under a dogwood tree in an area to the right of the entrance.

"I looked for you back there," he said.

"I can't get it out of my mind."

"I talked to a policeman."

"Because actually seeing it, I couldn't really grasp. It was so far-fetched. Seeing the child in that man's grip. I think it was more violent than guns. That poor woman watching it happen. How could she ever expect? I felt so weak and strange. I saw you coming along and I said I have to talk to someone. I know I just ranted."

"You were in complete control."

"I've been sitting here thinking there's no question about the elements. The car, the man, the mother, the child. Those are the parts. But how do the parts fit together? Because now that I've had some time to think, there's no explanation. A hole opened up in the air. That's how much sense it makes. There isn't a chance in a thousand I'll sleep tonight. It was all too awful, too enormous."

"She identified the man. It was definitely the father. She gave the police all the details. You had it just about totally right."

She looked at him carefully. He had a sudden sense of himself, rank and panting, cartoonish in orange shorts and a torn and faded top, and he felt a separation from the scene, as if he were watching from a place of concealment. She wore that odd pained smile. He backed up slightly, then leaned to shake her hand. This was how they said good night.

He went into the white lobby. The echo of the run hummed in his body. He stood waiting in a haze of weariness and thirst. The elevator arrived and the door slid open. He rode up alone through the heart of the building.

THE IVORY ACROBAT

When it was over she stood in the crowded street and listened to the dense murmur of all those people speaking. She heard the first distant blurt of car horns on the avenue. People studied each other to match reactions. She watched them search the street for faces, signs that so-and-so was safe. She realized the streetlights were on and tried to recall how long her flat had been dark. Everyone was talking. She heard the same phrases repeated and stood with her arms crossed on her chest, watching a woman carry a chair to a suitable spot. The sound of blowing horns drifted through the streets. People leaving the city in radial streams. Already she was thinking ahead to the next one. There's always supposed to be another, possibly many more.

The cardplayers stood outside the café, some of them inspecting a chunk of fallen masonry on the sidewalk, others looking toward the roof. Here and there a jutting face, a body slowly turning, searching. She wore what she'd been wearing when it started, jeans and shirt and light sweater, and it was night and winter, and funny-looking moccasins she only wore indoors. The horns grew louder in a kind of cry, an animal awe. The panic god is Greek after all. She thought about it again and wasn't sure the lights had been out at all. Women stood with arms folded in the cold. She walked along the middle of the street, listening to the voices, translating phrases to herself. It was the same for everyone. They said the same things and searched for faces. The streets were narrow here and people sat in parked cars, smoking. Here and there a child running, hand-shuffling through the crowd, excited children out near midnight. She thought there might be a glow in the sky and climbed a broad stepped street that had a vantage toward the gulf. She seemed to recall reading there's sometimes a light in the sky just before it happens or just after. This came under the heading of unexplained.

After a while they started going back inside. Kyle walked for three hours. She watched the cars push into major avenues that led to the mountains and the coast. Traffic lights were dark in certain areas. The long lines of cars, knotted and bent, made scant gains forward. Paralysis. She thought the scene resembled some landscape in the dreaming part of us, what the city teaches us to fear. They were pressing on the horns. The noise spread along the streets and reached a final mass denial, a desolation. It subsided after a time, then began to build again. She saw people sleeping on benches and families collected in cars parked on sidewalks and median strips. She recalled all the things she'd ever heard about an earthquake.

In her district the streets were almost empty now. She went into her building and took the stairs to five. The lights were on in her flat, and there were broken pieces of terracotta (she only now remembered) scattered on the floor by the bookcase. Long cracks branched along the west wall. She changed into walking shoes, put on a padded ski jacket and turned off the lights except for a lamp by the door. Then she placed herself on the sofa between a sheet and blanket, her head resting on an airline pillow. She closed her eyes and folded up, elbows at her midsection, hands pressed together between her knees. She tried to will herself to sleep but realized she was listening intently, listening to the room. She lay in a kind of timeless drift, a mindwork spiral, carried on half-formed thoughts. She passed into a false sleep and then was listening again. She opened her eyes. The clock read four-forty. She heard something that sounded like sand spilling, a trickle of gritty dust between the walls of abutting structures. The room began to move in a creaking sigh. Louder, powerfully. She was out of bed and on her way to the door, moving slightly crouched. She opened the door and stood under the lintel until the shaking stopped. She took the stairway down. No neighbors popping out of doors this time, bending arms into coats. The streets remained nearly empty and she guessed people didn't want to bother doing it again. She wandered well past daybreak. A few campfires burned in the parks. The horn-blowing was sporadic now. She walked around her building a number of times, finally sitting on a bench near the newspaper kiosk. She watched people enter the street to begin the day and she looked for something in their faces that might tell her what kind of night they'd spent. She was afraid everything would appear to be normal. She hated to think that people might easily resume the knockabout routine of frazzled Athens. She didn't want to be alone in her perception that something had basically changed. The world was narrowed down to inside and outside.

She had lunch with Edmund, a colleague at the little school where she taught music to children of the international

57

community, grades three to six. She was eager to hear how he'd reacted to the situation but first talked him into eating outdoors at a table set against the facade of a busy snack bar.

"We could still be killed," Edmund said, "by falling balconies. Or freeze in our chairs."

"How did you feel?"

"I thought my heart was going to jump right through my chest."

"Good. Me too."

"I fled."

"Of course."

"On my way down the stairs I had the oddest conversation with the man who lives across the hall. I mean we'd hardly said a word to each other before this. There were two dozen people barreling down the stairs. Suddenly he wanted to talk. He asked me where I work. Introduced me to his wife, who was pretty goddamn uninterested at that point in the details of my employment. He asked me how I like living in Greece."

Skies were low and gray. People called to each other on the street, chanted from passing cars. *Eksi komma eksi.* They were referring to the first one, the bigger one. Six point six. Kyle had been hearing the number all morning, spoken with reverence, anxiety, grim pride, an echo along the brooding streets, a form of fatalistic greeting.

"Then what?" she said.

"The second one. I woke up moments before."

"You heard something."

"Like a child tossing a handful of sand against the window."

"Very good," she said.

"Then it hit."

"It hit."

"Bang. I leaped out of bed like a madman."

"Did the lights go out?"

"No."

"What about the first time?"

"I'm not sure actually."

"Good. Neither am I. Was there a glow in the sky at any point?"

"Not that I noticed."

"We could be dealing with a myth here."

"The newspapers said a power station may have failed, causing a flash. There's confusion on this point."

"But we experienced similar things."

"It would appear," he said.

"Good. I'm glad."

She thought of him as the English Boy although he was thirty-six, divorced, apparently arthritic and not even English. But he felt the English rapture over Greek light, where all Kyle saw was chemical smoke lapping at the ruins. And he had the prim outdated face of a schoolboy in a formal portrait, wire-haired and pensive.

"Where was the epicenter?" she said.

"About forty miles west of here."

"The dead?"

"Thirteen and counting."

"What will we do?"

"About what?" he said.

"Everything. All the aftershocks."

"We've had two hundred already. It's expected to last many weeks. Read the papers. Months perhaps."

"Look, Edmund. I don't want to be alone tonight. Okay?"

*   *   *

She lived inside a pause. She was always pausing, alone in her flat, to listen. Her hearing developed a cleanness, a discriminating rigor. She sat at the small table where she ate her meals, listening. The room had a dozen sounds, mainly disturbances of tone, pressures releasing in the walls, and she followed them and waited. There was a second and safer level she reserved for street noises, the elevator rising. All the danger was inside.

A rustle. A soft sway. She crouched in the open doorway like an atomic child.

The tremors entered her bloodstream. She listened and waited. She couldn't sleep at night and caught odd moments in daytime, dozing in an unused room at the school. She dreaded going home. She watched the food in her plate and sometimes stood, carefully listening, ready to go, to get outside. There must be something funny in this somewhere, a person standing motionless over her food, leaning ever so slightly toward the door, fingertips at the table edge.

Is it true that before a major quake the dogs and cats run away? She thought she'd read somewhere that people in California habitually check the personal columns in newspapers to see if the number of lost dogs has increased noticeably. Or are we dealing with a myth here?

The wind made the shutters swing and bang. She listened to the edges of the room, the interfaces. She heard everything. She put a tote bag near the door for hasty exits — money, books, passport, letters from home. She heard the sound of the knife sharpener's bell.

She didn't read the papers but gathered that the tremors numbered in the eight hundreds by latest count and the dead added up to twenty now, with hotel rubble and tent cities near the epicenter and people living in open areas in parts of Athens, their buildings judged unsafe.

The cardplayers wore their coats indoors. She walked past the cut-back mulberry trees and through the street market and looked at the woman selling eggs and wondered what she could say to her that might make them both feel better, in her fairly decent Greek, shopping for bargains. A man held the elevator door but she waved him off politely and took the stairs. She walked into her flat, listening. The terrace canopies humped out in the wind, snapping hard. She wanted her life to be episodic again, unpremeditated. A foreigner anonymous—soft-footed, self-informed, content to occupy herself in random observation. She wanted to talk unimportantly to grandmothers and children in the streets of her working-class district.

She rehearsed her exit mentally. So many steps from the table to the door. So many stairs to the street. She thought if she pictured it beforehand, it might go more smoothly.

The lottery man cried, "Today, today."

She tried to read through the edgy nights, the times of dull-witted terror. There were rumors that these were not aftershocks at all but warnings of some deep disquiet in the continental trench, the massing of a force that would roll across the marble-hearted city and bring it to dust. She sat up and turned the pages, trying to disguise herself as someone who routinely reads for fifteen minutes before dropping into easy sleep.

It was not so bad in school, where she was ready to protect the young, to cover their bodies with her own.

The tremors lived in her skin and were part of every breath

she took. She paused over her food. A rustle. An easing reedy tilt. She stood and listened, alone with the shaking earth.

Edmund told her he'd bought a gift to replace the terra-cotta roof ornament she'd had propped against the wall above the bookcase, acanthus leaves radiating from the head of a sleepy-eyed Hermes, shattered in the first tremor.

"You won't miss your Hermes all that much. I mean it's everywhere, isn't it?"

"That's what I liked about it."

"You can easily get another. They're piled up for sale."

"It'll only get broken," she said, "when the next one hits."

"Let's change the subject."

"There's only one subject. That's the trouble. I used to have a personality. What am I now?"

"Try to understand it's over."

"I'm down to pure dumb canine instinct."

"Life is going on. People are going about their business."

"No, they're not. Not the same way. Just because they don't walk around moaning."

"There's nothing to moan about. It's finished."

"Doesn't mean they're not preoccupied. It's been less than a week. There are tremors all the time."

"Growing ever smaller," he said.

"Some are not so small. Some are definite attention-getters."

"Change the subject please."

They were standing just outside the school entrance and Kyle was watching a group of children climb aboard a bus for a trip to a museum outside the city. She knew she could count on the English Boy to be exasperated with her. He was dependable that way. She always knew the position he would take and could often anticipate the actual words, practically moving her lips in unison with his. He brought some stability to dire times.

"You used to be lithe."

"Look at me now," she said.

"Lumbering."

"I wear layers of clothing. I wear clothes and change-of-clothes simultaneously. Just to be ready."

"I can't afford a change of clothes," he said.

"I can't afford the dry cleaning."

"I often wonder how this happened to me."

"I live without a refrigerator and telephone and radio and shower curtain and what else. I keep butter and milk on the balcony."

"You're very quiet," he said then. "Everyone says so."

"Am I? Who?"

"How old are you by the way?"

"Now that we've spent a night together, you mean?"

"Spent a night. Exactly. One night used up in huddled conversation."

"Well it helped me. It made a difference really. It was the crucial night. Not that the others have been so cozy."

"You're welcome to return, you know. I sit there thinking. A lithe young woman flying across the city into my arms."

The children waved at them from the windows and Edmund did a wild-eyed mime of a bus driver caught in agitated traffic. She watched the lightsome faces glide away.

"You have nice color," she said.

"What does that mean?"

"Your cheeks are pink and healthy. My father used to say if I ate my vegetables I'd have rosy cheeks."

She waited for Edmund to ask, What did your mother used to say? Then they walked for the time that remained before afternoon classes. Edmund bought a ring of sesame bread and gave her half. He paid for things by opening his fist and letting the vendor sort among the coins. It proved to everyone that he was only passing through.

"You've heard the rumors," she said.

"Rubbish."

"The government is concealing seismic data."

"There is absolutely no scientific evidence that a great quake is imminent. Read the papers."

She took off the bulky jacket and swung it over her shoulder. She realized she wanted him to think she was slightly foolish, controlled by mass emotion. There was some comfort in believing the worst as long as this was the reigning persuasion. But she didn't want to submit completely. She walked along wondering if she was appealing to Edmund for staunch pronouncements that she could use against herself.

"Do you have an inner life?"

"I sleep," he said.

"That's not what I mean."

They ran across a stretch of avenue where cars accelerated to a racing clip. It felt good to shake out of her jittery skin. She kept running for half a block and then turned to watch him approach clutching his chest and moving on doddery legs, as if for the regalement of children. He could look a little bookish even capering.

They approached the school building.

"I wonder what your hair would be like if you let it grow out."

"I can't afford the extra shampoo," she said.

"I can't afford a haircut at regular intervals, quite seriously."

"I live without a piano."

"And this is a wretchedness to compare with no refrigerator?"

"You can ask that question because you don't know me. I live without a bed."

"Is this true?"

"I sleep on a secondhand sofa. It has the texture of a barnacled hull."

"Then why stay?" he said.

"I can't save enough to go anywhere else and I'm certainly not ready to go home. Besides I like it here. I'm sort of stranded but in a more or less willing way. At least until now. The trouble with now is that we could be anywhere. The only thing that matters is where we're standing when it hits."

He presented the gift then, lifting it out of his jacket pocket and unwrapping the sepia paper with a teasing show of suspense. It was a reproduction of an ivory figurine from Crete, a bull leaper, female, her body deftly extended with tapered feet nearing the topmost point of a somersaulting curve. Edmund explained that the young woman was in the act of vaulting over the horns of a charging bull. This was a familiar scene in Minoan art, found in frescoes, bronzes, clay seals, gold signet rings, ceremonial cups. Most often a young man, sometimes a woman gripping a bull's horns and swinging up and over, propelled by the animal's head jerk. He told her the original ivory figure was broken in half in 1926 and asked her if she wanted to know how this happened.

"Don't tell me. I want to guess."

"An earthquake. But the restoration was routine."

Kyle took the figure in her hand.

"A bull coming at full gallop? Is this possible?"

"I'm not inclined to question what was possible thirty-six hundred years ago."

"I don't know the Minoans," she said. "Were they that far back?"

"Yes, and farther than that, much farther."

"Maybe if the bull was firmly tethered."

"It's never shown that way," he said. "It's shown big and fierce and running and bucking."

"Do we have to believe something happened exactly the way it was shown by artists?"

"No. But I believe it. And even though this particular leaper isn't accompanied by a bull, we know from her position that this is what she's doing."

"She's bull-leaping."

"Yes."

"And she will live to tell it."

"She has lived. She is living. That's why I got this for you really. I want her to remind you of your hidden litheness."

"But you're the acrobat," Kyle said. "You're the loose-jointed one, performing in the streets."

"To remind you of your fluent buoyant former self."

"You're the jumper and heel clicker."

"My joints ache like hell actually."

"Look at the veins in her hand and arm."

"I got it cheap in the flea market."

"That makes me feel much better."

"It's definitely you," he said. "It must be you. Do we agree on this? Just look and feel. It's your magical true self, mass-produced."

Kyle laughed.

"Lean and supple and young," he said. "Throbbing with inner life."

She laughed. Then the school bell rang and they went inside.

She stood in the middle of the room, dressed except for shoes, slowly buttoning her blouse. She paused. She worked the button through the slit. Then she stood on the wood floor, listening.

They were now saying twenty-five dead, thousands homeless. Some people had abandoned undamaged buildings, preferring the ragged safety of life outdoors. Kyle could easily see how that might happen. She had the first passable night's sleep but continued to stay off elevators and out of movie theaters. The wind knocked loose objects off the back balconies. She listened and waited. She visualized her exit from the room.

Sulfur fell from the factory skies, staining the pavement, and a teacher at the school said it was sand blown north from Libya on one of those lovely desert winds.

She sat on the sofa in pajamas and socks reading a book on local flora. A blanket covered her legs. A half-filled glass of water sat on the end table. Her eyes wandered from the page. It was two minutes before midnight. She paused, looking off toward the middle distance. Then she heard it coming, an earth roar, a power moving on the air. She sat for a long second, deeply thoughtful, before throwing off the blanket. The moment burst around her. She rushed to the door and opened it, half aware of rattling lampshades and something wet. She gripped the edges of the door frame and faced into the room. Things were jumping up and down. She formed the categorical thought, *This one is the biggest yet.* The room was more or less a blur. There was a sense that it was on the verge of splintering. She felt the effect in her legs this time, a kind of hollowing out, a soft surrender to some illness. It was hard to believe, hard to believe it was lasting so long. She pushed her hands against the door frame, searching for a calmness in herself. She could almost see a picture of her mind, a vague gray oval, floating over the room. The shaking would not stop. There was an anger in it, a hammering demand. Her face showed the crumpled effort of a heavy lifter. It wasn't easy to know what was happening around her. She couldn't see things in the normal way. She could only see herself, bright-skinned, waiting for the room to fold over her.

Then it ended and she pulled some clothes over her pajamas and took the stairway down. She moved fast. She ran across the small lobby, brushing past a man lighting a cigarette at the door. People were coming into the street. She went half a block and stopped at the edge of a large group. She was breathing hard and her arms hung limp. Her first clear thought was that she'd have to go back inside sooner or later. She listened to the voices fall around her. She wanted to hear someone say this very thing, that the cruelty existed in time, that they were all unprotected in the drive of time. She told a woman she thought a water pipe had broken in her flat and the woman closed her eyes and rocked her heavy head. When will it all end? She told the woman she'd forgotten to grab her tote bag on her way out the door despite days of careful planning and she tried to give the story a rueful nuance, make it funny and faintly self-mocking. There must be something funny we can cling to. They stood there rocking their heads.

All up and down the street there were people lighting cigarettes. It was eight days since the first tremor, eight days and one hour.

She walked most of the night. At three a.m. she stopped in the square in front of the Olympic Stadium. There were parked cars and scores of people and she studied the faces and stood listening. Traffic moved slowly past. There was a curious double mood, a lonely reflectiveness at the center of all the talk, a sense that people were half absent from the eager seeking of company. She started walking again.

Eating breakfast in her flat at nine o'clock she felt the first sizable aftershock. The room leaned heavily. She rose from the table, eyes wet, and opened the door and crouched there, holding a buttered roll.

Wrong. The last one was not the biggest on the Richter. It was only six point two.

And she found out it hadn't lasted longer than the others. This was a mass illusion, according to the word at school.

And the water she'd seen or felt had not come from a broken pipe but from a toppled drinking glass on the table by the sofa.

And why did they keep occurring at night?

And where was the English Boy?

The drinking glass was intact but her paperback book on plant life was wet and furrowed.

She took the stairs up and down.

She kept the tote bag ready at the door.

She was deprived of sentiments, pretensions, expectations, textures.

The pitiless thing was time, threat of advancing time.

She was deprived of presumptions, persuasions, complications, lies, every braided arrangement that made it possible to live.

Stay out of movies and crowded halls. She was down to categories of sound, to self-admonishments and endless inner scrutinies.

She paused, alone, to listen.

She pictured her sensible exit from the room.

She looked for something in people's faces that might tell her their experience was just like hers, down to the smallest strangest turn of thought.

There must be something funny in this somewhere that we can use to get us through the night.

She heard everything.

She took catnaps at school.

She was deprived of the city itself. We could be anywhere, any lost corner of Ohio.

She dreamed of a mayfly pond skimmed with fallen blossoms.

Take the stairs everywhere. Take a table near the exit in cafés and tavernas.

The cardplayers sat in hanging smoke, making necessary motions only, somberly guarding their cards.

She learned that Edmund was in the north with friends, peering into monasteries.

She heard the surge of motorcycles on the hill.

She inspected the cracks in the west wall and spoke to the landlord, who closed his eyes and rocked his heavy head.

The wind caused a rustling somewhere very near.

She sat up at night with her book of water-stiffened pages,

trying to read, trying to escape the feeling that she was being carried helplessly toward some pitching instant in time.

The acanthus is a spreading perennial.

And everything in the world is either inside or outside.

She came across the figurine one day inside a desk drawer at the school, lying among cough drops and paper clips, in an office used as a teachers' lounge. She didn't even remember putting it there and felt the familiar clashing agencies of shame and defensiveness working in her blood—a body heat rising against the reproach of forgotten things. She picked it up, finding something remarkable in the leaper's clean and open motion, in the detailed tension of forearms and hands. Shouldn't something so old have a formal bearing, a stiffness of figure? This was easy-flowing work. But beyond this surprise, there was little to know. She didn't know the Minoans. She wasn't even sure what the thing was made of, what kind of lightweight imitation ivory. It occurred to her that she'd left the figure in the desk because she didn't know what to do with it, how to underpin or prop it. The body was alone in space, with no supports, no fixed position, and seemed best suited to the palm of the hand.

She stood in the small room, listening.

Edmund had said the figure was like her. She studied it, trying to extract the sparest recognition. A girl in a loin-cloth and wristbands, double-necklaced, suspended over the horns of a running bull. The act, the leap itself, might be vaudeville or sacred terror. There were themes and secrets and storied lore in this six-inch figure that Kyle could not begin to guess at. She turned the object in her hand. All

71

the facile parallels fell away. Lithe, young, buoyant, modern; rumbling bulls and quaking earth. There was nothing that might connect her to the mind inside the work, an ivory carver, 1600 BC, moved by forces remote from her. She remembered the old earthen Hermes, flower-crowned, looking out at her from a knowable past, some shared theater of being. The Minoans were outside all this. Narrow-waisted, graceful, other-minded—lost across vales of language and magic, across dream cosmologies. This was the piece's little mystery. It was a thing in opposition, defining what she was not, marking the limits of the self. She closed her fist around it firmly and thought she could feel it beat against her skin with a soft and periodic pulse, an earthliness.

She was motionless, with tilted head, listening. Buses rolled past, sending diesel fumes through seams in the window frame. She looked toward a corner of the room, concentrating tightly. She listened and waited.

Her self-awareness ended where the acrobat began. Once she realized this, she put the object in her pocket and took it everywhere.

THE ANGEL
ESMERALDA

The old nun rose at dawn, feeling pain in every joint. She'd been rising at dawn since her days as a postulant, kneeling on hardwood floors to pray. First she raised the shade. That's the world out there, little green apples and infectious disease. Banded light fell across the room, steeping the tissued grain of the wood in an antique ocher glow so deeply pleasing in pattern and coloration that she had to look away or become girlishly engrossed. She knelt in the folds of the white night-gown, fabric endlessly laundered, beaten with swirled soap, left gristled and stiff. And the body beneath, the spindly thing she carried through the world, chalk pale mostly, and speck-led hands with high veins, and cropped hair that was fine and flaxy gray, and her bluesteel eyes—many a boy and girl of old saw those peepers in their dreams. She made the sign of the cross, murmuring the congruous words. *Amen*, an olden word, back to Greek and Hebrew, verily—touching her mid-section to complete the body-shaped cross. The briefest of everyday prayers yet carrying three years' indulgence, seven if you dip your hand in holy water before you mark the body. Prayer is a practical strategy, the gaining of temporal advan-tage in the capital markets of Sin and Remission.

She said a morning offering and got to her feet. At the sink she scrubbed her hands repeatedly with coarse brown soap. How can the hands be clean if the soap is not? This question was insistent in her life. But if you clean the soap with bleach, what do you clean the bleach bottle with? If you use scouring powder on the bleach bottle, how do you clean the box of Ajax? Germs have personalities. Different objects harbor threats of various insidious types. And the questions turn inward forever.

An hour later she was in her veil and habit, sitting in the passenger seat of a black van that was headed south out of the school district and down past the monster concrete expressway into the lost streets, a squander of burned-out buildings and unclaimed souls. Grace Fahey was at the wheel, a young nun in secular dress. All the nuns at the convent wore plain blouses and skirts except for Sister Edgar, who had permission from the motherhouse to fit herself out in the old things with the arcane names, the wimple, cincture and guimpe. She knew there were stories about her past, how she used to twirl the big-beaded rosary and crack students across the mouth with the iron crucifix. Things were simpler then. Clothing was layered, life was not. But Edgar stopped hitting kids years ago, even before she grew too old to teach. She knew the sisters whispered deliciously about her strictness, feeling shame and awe together. Such an open show of power in a bird-bodied soap-smelling female. Edgar stopped hitting children when the neighborhood changed and the faces of her students became darker. All the righteous fury went out of her soul. How could she strike a child who was not like her?

"The old jalop needs a tune-up," Gracie said. "Hear that noise?"

"Ask Ismael to take a look."

"Ku-ku-ku-ku."

"He's the expert."

"I can do it myself. I just need the right tools."

"I don't hear anything," Edgar said.

"Ku-ku-ku-ku? You don't hear that?"

"Maybe I'm going deaf."

"I'll go deaf before you do, Sister."

"Look, another angel on the wall."

The two women looked across a landscape of vacant lots filled with years of stratified deposits—the age-of-house garbage, the age-of-construction debris and vandalized car bodies. Many ages layered in waste. This area was called the Bird in jocular police parlance, short for bird sanctuary, a term that referred in this case to a tuck of land sitting adrift from the social order. Weeds and trees grew amid the dumped objects. There were dog packs, sightings of hawks and owls. City workers came periodically to excavate the site, the hoods of their sweatshirts fitted snug under their hard hats, and they stood warily by the great earth machines, the pumpkin-mudded backhoes and dozers, like infantrymen huddled near advancing tanks. But soon they left, they always left with holes half dug, pieces of equipment discarded, styrofoam cups, pepperoni pizzas. The nuns looked across all this. There were networks of vermin, craters chocked with plumbing fixtures and sheetrock. There were hillocks of slashed tires laced with thriving vine. Gunfire sang at sunset off the low walls of demolished buildings. The nuns sat in the van and looked. At the far end was a lone standing structure, a derelict tenement with an exposed wall where another building had once abutted. This wall was where Ismael Muñoz and his crew of graffiti writers spray-painted a memorial angel every time a child died in the neighborhood. Angels in blue and pink covered roughly half the high slab. The child's name and age were printed in cartoon bubbles under each angel, sometimes with cause of death or personal comments by the family, and as the van drew closer Edgar could see entries for TB, AIDS, beatings, drive-by shootings, blood disorders, measles, general neglect and abandonment at birth—left in dumpster, forgot in car, left in Glad bag Xmas Eve.

"I wish they'd stop already with the angels," Gracie said. "It's in totally bad taste. A fourteenth-century church, that's where you go for angels. This wall publicizes all the things we're working to change. Ismael should look for positive things to emphasize. The townhouses, the community gardens that people plant. The townhouses are nice, they're clean. Walk around the corner, you see ordinary people going to work, going to school. Stores and churches."

"Titanic Power Baptist Church."

"It's a church, it's a church, what's the difference? The area's full of churches. Decent working people. Ismael wants to do a wall, these are the people he should celebrate. Be positive."

Edgar laughed inside her skull. It was the drama of the angels that made her feel she belonged here. It was the terrible death these angels represented. It was the danger the writers faced to produce their graffiti. There were no fire escapes or windows on the memorial wall and the writers had to rappel from the roof with belayed ropes or sway on makeshift scaffolds when they did an angel in the lower ranks. Ismael spoke of a companion wall for dead graffitists, flashing his wasted smile.

"And he does pink for girls and blue for boys. That really sets my teeth on edge."

"There are other colors," Edgar said.

"Sure, the streamers that the angels hold aloft. Big ribbons in the sky. Makes me want to be sick in the street."

They stopped at the friary to pick up food they would distribute to the needy. The friary was an old brick building wedged between boarded tenements. Three monks in gray cloaks and rope belts worked in an anteroom, getting the day's shipment ready. Grace, Edgar and Brother Mike carried the plastic bags out to the van. Mike was an ex-fireman with a Brillo beard and wispy ponytail. He looked like two different guys front and back. When the nuns first appeared he'd offered to serve as guide, a protecting presence, but Edgar had firmly declined. She believed her habit and veil were safety enough. Beyond these South Bronx streets, people might look at her and think she existed outside history and chronology. But inside the strew of rubble she was a natural sight, she and the robed monks. What figures could be so timely, costumed for rats and plague?

Edgar liked seeing the monks in the street. They visited the homebound, ran a shelter for the homeless; they collected food for the hungry. And they were men in a place where few men remained. Teenage boys in clusters, armed drug dealers—these were the men of the immediate streets. She didn't know where the others had gone, the fathers, living with second or third families, hidden in rooming houses or sleeping under highways in refrigerator boxes, buried in the potter's field on Hart Island.

"I'm counting plant species," Brother Mike said. "I've got a book I take out to the lots."

Gracie said, "You stay on the fringes, right?"

"They know me in the lots."

"Who knows you? The dogs know you? There are rabid dogs, Mike."

"I'm a Franciscan, okay? Birds light on my index finger."

"Stay on the fringes," Gracie told him.

"There's a girl I keep seeing, maybe twelve years old, runs away when I try to talk to her. I get the feeling she's living in the ruins. Ask around."

"Will do," Gracie said.

When the van was loaded they drove back to the Bird to do their business with Ismael and to pick up a few of his crew who would help them distribute the food. What was their business with Ismael? They gave him lists that detailed the locations of abandoned cars in the North Bronx, particularly along the Bronx River, which was a major dump site for stolen joyridden semistripped gas-siphoned pariah-dog vehicles. Ismael sent his crew to collect the car bodies and whatever parts might remain unrelinquished. They used a small flatbed truck with an undependable winch and a motif of souls-in-hell graffiti on the cab, deck and mudflaps. The car hulks came here to the lots for inspection and price-setting by Ismael and were then delivered to a scrap-metal operation in remotest Brooklyn. Sometimes there were forty or fifty cannibalized car bodies dumped in the lots, museum-quality—bashed and rusted, hoodless, doorless, windows deep-streaked like starry nights in the mountains.

When the van approached the building, Edgar felt along her midsection for the latex gloves she kept tucked in her belt.

Ismael had teams of car spotters who ranged across the

boroughs, concentrating on the bleak streets under bridges and viaducts. Charred cars, upside-down cars, cars with dead bodies wrapped in shower curtains all available for salvage inside the city limits. The money he paid the nuns for their locational work went to the friary for groceries.

Gracie parked the van, the only operating vehicle in human sight. She attached the vinyl-coated steel collar to the steering wheel, fitting the rod into the lock housing. At the same time Edgar force-fitted the latex gloves onto her hands, feeling the secret reassurance of synthetic things, adhesive rubberized plastic, a shield against organic menace, the spurt of blood or pus and the viral entities hidden within, submicroscopic parasites in their protein coats.

Squatters occupied a number of floors. Edgar didn't need to see them to know who they were. They were a civilization of indigents subsisting without heat, lights or water. They were nuclear families with toys and pets, junkies who roamed at night in dead men's Reeboks. She knew who they were through assimilation, through the ingestion of messages that riddled the streets. They were foragers and gatherers, can-redeemers, the people who yawed through subway cars with paper cups. And doxies sunning on the roof in clement weather and men with warrants outstanding for reckless endangerment and depraved indifference and other offenses requiring the rounded Victorian locutions that modern courts have adopted to match the woodwork. And shouters of the Spirit, she knew this for a fact—a band of charismatics who leaped and wept on the top floor, uttering words and nonwords, treating knife wounds with prayer.

Ismael had his headquarters on three and the nuns hustled up the stairs. Grace had a tendency to look back unnecessarily at the senior nun, who ached in her movable parts but kept pace well enough, her habit whispering through the stairwell.

"Needles on the landing," Gracie warned.

Watch the needles, sidestep the needles, such deft instruments of self-disregard. Gracie couldn't understand why an addict would not be sure to use clean needles. This failure made her pop her cheeks in anger. But Edgar thought about the lure of damnation, the little love bite of that dragonfly dagger. If you know you're worth nothing, only a gamble with death can gratify your vanity.

Ismael stood barefoot on dusty floorboards in a pair of old chinos rolled to his calves and a bright shirt worn outside his pants and he resembled some carefree Cuban ankle-wading in happy surf.

"Sisters, what do you have for me?"

Edgar thought he was quite young despite the seasoned air, maybe early thirties—scattered beard, a sweet smile complicated by rotting teeth. Members of his crew stood around smoking, uncertain of the image they wanted to convey. He sent two of them down to watch the van and the food. Edgar knew that Gracie did not trust these kids. Graffiti writers, car scavengers, probably petty thieves, maybe worse. All street, no home or school. Edgar's basic complaint was their English. They spoke an unfinished English, soft and muffled, insufficiently suffixed, and she wanted to drum some hard g's into the ends of their gerunds.

Gracie handed over a list of cars they'd spotted in the last few days. Details of time and place, type of vehicle, condition of same.

He said, "You do nice work. My other people do like this, we run the world by now."

What was Edgar supposed to do, correct their grammar and pronunciation, kids suffering from malnutrition, unparented some of them, some visibly pregnant—there were at least four girls in the crew. In fact she was inclined to do just that. She wanted to get them in a room with a blackboard and to buzz their minds with Spelling and Punctuation, transitive verbs, *i* before *e* except after *c*. She wanted to drill them in the lessons of the old Baltimore Catechism. True or false, yes or no, fill in the blanks. She'd talked to Ismael about this and he'd made an effort to look interested, nodding heavily and muttering insincere assurances that he would think about the matter.

"I can pay you next time," Ismael said. "I got some things I'm doing that I need the capital."

"What things?" Gracie said.

"I'm making plans I get some heat and electric in here, plus pirate cable for the Knicks."

Edgar stood at the far end of the room, by a window facing front, and she saw someone moving among the poplars and ailanthus trees in the most overgrown part of the rubbled lots. A girl in a too-big jersey and striped pants grubbing in the underbrush, maybe for something to eat or wear. Edgar watched her, a lanky kid who had a sort of feral intelligence, a sureness of gesture and step—she looked helpless but alert, she looked unwashed but completely clean somehow, earthclean and hungry and quick. There was something about her that mesmerized the nun, a charmed quality, a grace that guided and sustained.

Edgar said something and just then the girl slipped

DON DeLILLO

through a maze of wrecked cars and by the time Gracie reached the window she was barely a flick of the eye, lost in the low ruins of an old firehouse.

"Who is this girl," Gracie said, "who's out there in the lots, hiding from people?"

Ismael looked at his crew and one of them piped up, an undersized boy in spray-painted jeans, dark-skinned and shirtless.

"Esmeralda. Nobody know where her mother's at."

Gracie said, "Can you find the girl and then tell Brother Mike?"

"This girl she being swift."

A little murmur of assent.

"She be a running fool this girl."

Titters, brief.

"Why did her mother go away?"

"She be a addict. They un, you know, predictable."

If you let me teach you not to end a sentence with a preposition, Edgar thought, I will save your life.

Ismael said, "Maybe the mother returns. She feels the worm of remorse. You have to think positive."

"I do," Gracie said. "All the time."

"But the truth of the matter there's kids that are better off without their mothers or fathers. Because their mothers or fathers are dangering their safety."

Gracie said, "If anyone sees Esmeralda, take her to Brother Mike or hold her, I mean really hold her until I can get here and talk to her. She's too young to be on her own or even living with the crew. Brother said she's twelve."

"Twelve is not so young," Ismael said. "One of my best

82

writers, he does wildstyle, he's exactly twelve more or less. Juano. I send him down in a rope for the complicated letters."

"When do we get our money?" Gracie said.

"Next time for sure. I make practically, you know, nothing on this scrap. My margin it's very minimum. I'm looking to expand outside Brooklyn. Sell my cars to one of these up-and-coming countries that's making the bomb."

"Making the what? I don't think they're looking for junked cars," Gracie said. "I think they're looking for weapons-grade uranium."

"The Japanese built their navy with the Sixth Avenue el. You know this story? One day it's scrap, next day it's a plane taking off a deck. Hey, don't be surprise my scrap ends up in North, you know, Korea."

Edgar caught the smirk on Gracie's face. Edgar did not smirk. This was not a subject she could ever take lightly. Edgar was a cold-war nun who'd once lined the walls of her room with aluminum foil as a shield against nuclear fallout from Communist bombs. Not that she didn't think a war might be thrilling. She daydreamed many a domed flash in the film of her skin, tried to conjure the burst even now, with the USSR crumbled alphabetically, the massive letters toppled like Cyrillic statuary.

They went down to the van, the nuns and three kids, and with the two kids already on the street they set out to distribute the food, starting with the hardest cases in the projects.

They rode the elevators and walked down the long passageways. Behind each door a set of unimaginable lives, with histories and memories, pet fish swimming in dusty bowls. Edgar led the way, the five kids in single file behind her, each with two bags of food, and Gracie at the rear, carrying food, calling out apartment numbers of people on the list.

They spoke to an elderly woman who lived alone, a diabetic with an amputated leg.

They saw a man with epilepsy.

They spoke to two blind women who lived together and shared a seeing-eye dog.

They saw a woman in a wheelchair who wore a FUCK NEW YORK T-shirt. Gracie said she would probably trade the food they gave her for heroin, the dirtiest street scag available. The crew looked on, frowning. Gracie set her jaw, she narrowed her pale eyes and handed over the food anyway. They argued about this, not just the nuns but the crew as well. It was Sister Grace against everybody. Even the wheelchair woman didn't think she should get the food.

They saw a man with cancer who tried to kiss the latexed hands of Sister Edgar.

They saw five small children bunched on a bed being minded by a ten-year-old.

They went down the passageways. The kids returned to the van for more food and they went single-file down the passageways in the bleached light.

They talked to a pregnant woman watching a soap opera in Spanish. Edgar told her if a child dies after being baptized, she goes straight to heaven. The woman was impressed. If a child is in danger and there is no priest, Edgar said, the woman herself can administer baptism. How? Pour ordinary water on the forehead of the child, saying, "I baptize thee in the name of the Father and of the Son and of the Holy Ghost." The woman repeated the words in Spanish and English and everyone felt better.

They went down the passageways past a hundred closed doors and Edgar thought of all the infants in limbo, unbaptized, babies in the seminether, hell-bordered, and the nonbabies of abortion, a cosmic cloud of slushed fetuses floating in the rings of Saturn, or babies born without immune systems, bubble children raised by computer, or babies born addicted—she saw them all the time, bulb-headed newborns with crack habits, they resembled something out of peasant folklore.

They heard garbage crashing down the incinerator chutes and they walked one behind the other, three boys and two girls forming one body with the nuns, a single sway-backed figure with many moving parts. They rode the elevators down and finished their deliveries in a group of tenements where boards replaced broken glass in the lobby doors.

Gracie dropped the crew at the Bird just as a bus pulled up. What's this, do you believe it? A tour bus in carnival colors with a sign in the slot above the windshield reading SOUTH BRONX SURREAL. Gracie's breathing grew intense. About thirty Europeans with slung cameras stepped shyly onto the sidewalk in front of the boarded shops and closed factories and they gazed across the street at the derelict tenement in the middle distance.

Gracie went half berserk, sticking her head out of the van and calling, "It's not surreal. It's real, it's real. You're making it surreal by coming here. Your bus is surreal. You're surreal."

A monk rode by on a rickety bike. The tourists watched him pedal up the street. They listened to Gracie shout at them. They saw a man come along with battery-run pinwheels he was selling, brightly colored vanes pinned to a stick, and he held a dozen or so in his hands with others jutting from his pockets and clutched under his arms, plastic vanes spinning all around him—an elderly black fellow in a yellow skullcap. They saw this man. They saw the ailanthus jungle and the smash heap of mortified cars and they looked at the six-story slab of painted angels with streamers rippled above their cherub heads.

Gracie shouting, "This is real, it's real." Shouting, "Brussels is surreal. Milan is surreal. This is the only real. The Bronx is real."

A tourist bought a pinwheel and got back in the bus. Gracie pulled away muttering. In Europe the nuns wear bonnets like cantilevered beach houses. That's surreal, she said. A traffic jam developed not far from the Bird. The two women sat with drifting thoughts. Edgar watched children walk home from school, breathing air that rises from the oceans and comes windborne to this street at the edge of the continent. Woe betide the child with dirty fingernails. She used to drum the knuckles of her fifth-graders with a ruler if their hands were not bright as minted dimes.

A clamor rising all around them, weary beeping horns and police sirens and the great saurian roar of fire-engine klaxons.

"Sister, sometimes I wonder why you put up with all this," Gracie said. "You've earned some peace and quiet. You could live upstate and do development work for the order. How I would love to sit in the rose garden with a mystery novel and old Pepper curled at my feet." Old Pepper was the cat in the motherhouse upstate. "You could take a picnic lunch to the pond."

Edgar had a mirthless inner grin that floated somewhere back near her palate. She did not yearn for life upstate. This was the truth of the world, right here, her soul's own home, herself—she saw herself, the fraidy child who must face the real terror of the streets to cure the linger of destruction inside her. Where else would she do her work but under the brave and crazy wall of Ismael Muñoz?

Then Gracie was out of the van. She was out of the seat belt, out of the van and running down the street. The door hung open. Edgar understood at once. She turned and saw the girl, Esmeralda, half a block ahead of Gracie, running for the Bird. Gracie moved among the cars in her clunky shoes and frump skirt. She followed the girl around a corner where the tour bus sat dead in traffic. The tourists watched the running figures. Edgar could see their heads turn in unison, pinwheels spinning at the windows.

All sounds gathered in the dimming sky.

She thought she understood the tourists. You travel somewhere not for museums and sunsets but for ruins, bombed-out terrain, for the moss-grown memory of torture and war. Emergency vehicles were massing about a block and a half away. She saw workers pry open subway gratings in billows of pale smoke and she said a fast prayer, an act of hope, three years' indulgence. Then heads and torsos began to emerge, indistinctly, people coming into the air with jaws skewed open in frantic gasps. A short circuit, a subway fire. Through the rearview mirror she spotted tourists getting off the bus and edging along the street, poised to take pictures. And the schoolkids going by, barely interested—they saw tapes of actual killings on TV. But what did she know, an old woman who ate fish on Friday and longed for the Latin mass? She was far less worthy than Sister Grace. Gracie was a soldier, a fighter for human worth. Edgar was basically a junior G-man, protecting a set of laws and prohibitions. She heard the yammer of police cars pulsing in stalled traffic and saw a hundred subway riders come out of the tunnels accompanied by workers in incandescent vests and she watched the tourists snapping pictures and thought of the trip she'd made to Rome many years ago, for study and spiritual renewal, and she'd swayed beneath the great domes and prowled the catacombs and church basements and this is what she thought as the riders came up to the street, how she'd stood in a subterranean chapel in a Capuchin church and could not take her eyes off the skeletons stacked there, wondering about the monks whose flesh had once decorated these metatarsals and femurs and skulls, many skulls heaped in alcoves and catty-corners, and she remembered thinking vindictively that these are the dead who will come out of the earth to lash and cudgel the living, to punish the sins of the living—death, yes, triumphant—but does she really want to believe that, still?

Gracie edged into the driver's seat, unhappy and flushed.

"Nearly caught her. We ran into the thickest part of the lots and then I was distracted, damn scared actually, because bats, I couldn't believe it, actual bats—like the only flying mammals on earth?" She made ironic wing motions with her fingers. "They came swirling up out of a crater filled with medical waste. Bandages smeared with body fluids."

"I don't want to hear it," Edgar said.

"I saw, like, enough used syringes to satisfy the death wish of entire cities. Dead white mice by the hundreds with stiff flat bodies. You could flip them like baseball cards."

Edgar stretched her fingers inside the milky gloves.

"And Esmeralda somewhere in those shrubs and junked

cars. I'll bet anything she's living in a car," Gracie said. "What happened here? Subway fire, looks like."

"Yes."

"Any dead?"

"I don't think so."

"I wish I'd caught her."

"She'll be all right," Edgar said.

"She won't be all right."

"She can take care of herself. She knows the landscape. She's smart."

"Sooner or later," Gracie said.

"She's safe. She's smart. She'll be all right."

And that night, under the first tier of scratchy sleep, Edgar saw the subway riders once again, adult males, females of childbearing age, all rescued from the smoky tunnels, groping along catwalks and led up companion ladders to the street—fathers and mothers, the lost parents found and gathered, shirt-plucked and bodied up, guided to the surface by small faceless figures with Day-Glo wings.

And some weeks later Edgar and Grace made their way on foot across a patch of leaf rot to the banks of the Bronx River near the city limits where a rear-ended Honda sat discarded in underbrush, plates gone, tires gone, windows lifted cleanly, rats ascratch in the glove compartment, and after they noted the particulars of abandonment and got back in the van, Edgar had an awful feeling, one of those forebodings from years long past when she sensed dire things about a pupil or a parent or another nun and felt stirrings of information in the dusty corridors of the convent or the school's supply room that smelled of pencil wood and composition books or the church that abutted the school, some dark knowledge in the smoke that floated from the altar boy's swinging censer, because things used to come to her in the creak of old floorboards and the odor of clothes, other people's damp camel coats, because she drew News and Rumors and Catastrophes into the spotless cotton pores of her habit and veil.

Not that she claimed the power to live without doubt.

She doubted and she cleaned. That night she leaned over the washbasin in her room and cleaned every bristle of the scrub brush with steel wool drenched in disinfectant. But this meant she had to immerse the bottle of disinfectant in something stronger than disinfectant. And she hadn't done this. She hadn't done it because the regression was infinite. And the regression was infinite because it is called infinite regression. You see how doubt becomes a disease that spreads beyond the pushy extrusions of matter and into the elevated spaces where words play upon themselves.

And another morning a day later. She sat in the van and watched Sister Grace emerge from the convent, the rolling gait, the short legs and squarish body, Gracie's face averted as she edged around the front of the vehicle and opened the door on the driver's side.

She got in and gripped the wheel, looking straight ahead.

"I got a call from the friary."

Then she reached for the door and shut it. She gripped the wheel again.

"Somebody raped Esmeralda and threw her off a roof."

She started the engine.

"I'm sitting here thinking, Who do I kill?"

She looked at Edgar briefly, then put the van in gear.

"Because who do I kill is the only question I can ask myself without falling apart completely."

They drove south through local streets, the tenement brick smoked mellow in the morning light. Edgar felt the weather of Gracie's rage and pain—she'd approached the girl two or three times in recent weeks, had talked to her from a distance, thrown a bag of clothing into the pokeweed where Esmeralda stood. They rode all the way in silence with the older nun mind-reciting questions and answers from the Baltimore Catechism. The strength of these exercises, which were a form of perdurable prayer, lay in the voices that accompanied hers, children responding through the decades, syllable-crisp, a panpipe chant that was the lucid music of her life. Question and answer. What deeper dialogue might right minds devise? She reached her hand across to Gracie's on the wheel and kept it there for a digital tick on the dashboard clock. Who made us? God made us. Those clear-eyed faces so believing. Who is God? God is the Supreme Being who made all things. She felt tired in her arms, her arms were heavy and dead and she got all the way to Lesson 12 when the projects appeared at the rim of the sky, upper windows white with sunplay against the broad dark face of beaten stone.

When Gracie finally spoke she said, "It's still there."

"What's still there?"

"Hear it, hear it?"

"Hear what?" Edgar said.

"Ku-ku-ku-ku."

Then she drove the van down past the projects toward the painted wall.

When they got there the angel was already sprayed in

place. They gave her a pink sweatshirt and pink and aqua pants and a pair of white Air Jordans with the logo prominent—she was a running fool, so Ismael gave her running shoes. And the little kid named Juano still dangled from a rope, winched down from the roof by the old hand-powered hoist they used to grapple cars onto the deck of the truck. Ismael and others bent over the ledge, attempting to shout correct spellings down to him as he drifted to and from the wall, leaning in to spray the interlaced letters that marked the great gone era of wildstyle graffiti. The nuns stood outside the van, watching the kid finish the last scanted word and then saw him yanked skyward in the cutting wind.

ESMERALDA LOPEZ

12 YEAR

PETECTED IN HEVEN

They all met on the third floor and Gracie paced the hollow room. Ismael stood in a corner smoking a Phillies Blunt. The nun did not seem to know where to begin, how to address the nameless thing that someone had done to this child she'd so hoped to save. She paced, she clenched her fists. They heard the gassy moan of a city bus some blocks away.

"Ismael. You have to find out who this guy is that did this thing."

"You think I'm running here? El Lay Pee Dee?"

"You have contacts in the neighborhood that no one else has."

"What neighborhood? The neighborhood's over there. This here's the Bird. It's all I can do to get these kids so they spell a word on the freaking wall. When I was writing we did subway cars in the dark without a letter misspell."

"Who cares about spelling?" Gracie said.

Ismael exchanged a secret look with Sister Edgar, giving her a snaggle smile from out of his history of dental neglect. She felt weak and lost. Now that Terror has become local, how do we live? she thought. The great thrown shadow dismantled—no longer a launched object in the sky named for a Greek goddess on a bell krater in 500 BC. What is Terror now? Some noise on the pavement very near, a thief with a paring knife or the stammer of casual rounds from a passing car. Someone who carries off your child. Ancient fears called back, they will steal my child, they will come into my house when I'm asleep and cut out my heart because they have a dialogue with Satan. She let Gracie carry her grief and fatigue for the rest of that day and the day after and the two or three weeks after that. Edgar thought she might fall into crisis, begin to see the world as a spurt of blank matter that chanced to make an emerald planet here and a dead star there, with random waste between. The serenity of immense design was missing from her sleep, form and proportion, the power that awes and thrills. When Gracie and the crew took food into the projects, Edgar waited in the van, she was the nun in the van, unable to face the people who needed reasons for Esmeralda.

Mother of Mercy pray for us. Three hundred days.

Then the stories began, word passing block to block, moving through churches and superettes, maybe garbled slightly, mistranslated here and there, but not deeply distorted—it was clear enough that people were talking about the same uncanny occurrence. And some of them went and looked and told others, stirring the hope that grows on surpassing things.

They gathered after dusk at a windy place between bridge approaches, seven or eight people drawn by the word of one or two, then thirty people drawn by the seven, then a tight silent crowd that grew bigger but no less respectful, two hundred people wedged onto a traffic island in the bottommost Bronx where the expressway arches down from the terminal market and the train yards stretch toward the narrows, all that industrial desolation that breaks your heart with its fretful Depression beauty—the ramps that shoot tall weeds and the old railroad bridge spanning the Harlem River, an openwork tower at either end, maybe swaying slightly in persistent wind.

Wedged, they came and parked their cars if they had cars, six or seven to a car, parking tilted on a high shoulder or in the factory side streets, and they wedged themselves onto the concrete island between the expressway and the pocked boulevard, feeling the wind come chilling in and gazing above the wash of madcap traffic to a billboard floating in the gloom—an advertising sign scaffolded high above the riverbank and meant to attract the doped-over glances of commuters on the trains that ran incessantly down from the northern suburbs into the thick of Manhattan money and glut.

Edgar sat across from Gracie in the refectory. She ate her food without tasting it because she'd decided years ago that taste was not the point. The point was to clean the plate.

Gracie said, "No, please, you can't."

"Just to see."

"No, no, no, no."

"I want to see for myself."

"This is tabloid. This is the worst kind of tabloid superstition. It's horrible. A complete, what is it? A complete abdication, you know? Be sensible. Don't abdicate your good sense."

"It could be her they're seeing."

"You know what this is? It's the nightly news. It's the local news at eleven with all the grotesque items neatly spaced to keep you watching the whole half hour."

"I think I have to go," Edgar said.

"This is something for poor people to confront and judge and understand if they can and we have to see it in that framework. The poor need visions, okay?"

"I believe you are patronizing the people you love," Edgar said softly.

"That's not fair."

"You say the poor. But who else would saints appear to? Do saints and angels appear to bank presidents? Eat your carrots."

"It's the nightly news. It's gross exploitation of a child's horrible murder."

"But who is exploiting? No one's exploiting," Edgar said. "People go there to weep, to believe."

"It's how the news becomes so powerful it doesn't need TV or newspapers. It exists in people's perceptions. It becomes real or fake-real so people think they're seeing reality when they're seeing something they invent. It's the news without the media."

Edgar ate her bread.

"I'm older than the pope. I never thought I would live long enough to be older than a pope and I think I need to see this thing."

"Pictures lie," Gracie said.

"I think I need to see it."

"Don't pray to pictures, pray to saints."

"I think I need to go."

"But you can't. It's crazy. Don't go, Sister."

But Edgar went. She went with a shy quiet type named Janis Loudermilk, who wore a retainer for spacey teeth. They took the bus and subway and walked the last three blocks and Sister Jan carried a portable phone in case they needed aid.

A madder orange moon hung over the city.

People in the glare of passing cars, hundreds clustered on the island, their own cars parked cockeyed and biaswise, dangerously near the streaming traffic. The nuns dashed across the boulevard and squeezed onto the island and people made room for them, pressed bodies apart to let them stand at ease.

They followed the crowd's stoked gaze. They stood and looked. The billboard was unevenly lighted, dim in spots, several bulbs blown and unreplaced, but the central elements were clear, a vast cascade of orange juice pouring diagonally from top right into a goblet that was handheld at lower left—the perfectly formed hand of a female Caucasian of the middle suburbs. Distant willows and a vaguish lake view set the social locus. But it was the juice that commanded the eye, thick and pulpy with a ruddled flush that matched the madder moon. And the first detailed drops plashing at the bottom of the goblet with a scatter of spindrift, each fleck embellished like the figurations of a precisionist epic. What a lavishment of effort and technique, no refinement spared—the equivalent, Edgar thought, of medieval church architecture.

And the six-ounce cans of Minute Maid arrayed across the bottom of the board, a hundred identical cans so familiar in design and color and typeface that they had personality, the convivial cuteness of little orange people.

Edgar didn't know how long they were supposed to wait or exactly what was supposed to happen. Produce trucks passed in the rumbling dusk. She let her eyes wander to the crowd. Working people, she thought. Working women, shopkeepers, maybe some drifters and squatters but not many, and then she noticed a group near the front, fitted snug to the prowed shape of the island—they were the charismatics from the top floor of the tenement in the Bird, dressed mainly in floppy white, tublike women, reedy men with dreadlocks. The crowd was patient, she was not, finding herself taut with misgiving, hearing Gracie in her head. Planes dropped out of the darkness toward La Guardia, splitting the air with throttled booms. She and Sister Jan traded a sad glance. They stood and looked. They stared stupidly at the juice. After twenty minutes there was a rustle, a sort of human wind, and people looked north, children pointed north, and Edgar strained to catch what they were seeing.

The train.

She felt the words before she saw the object. She felt the words although no one had spoken them. This is how a crowd brings things to single consciousness. Then she saw it, an ordinary commuter train, silver and blue, ungraffitied, moving smoothly toward the drawbridge. The headlights swept the billboard and she heard a sound from the crowd, a gasp that shot into sobs and moans and the cry of some unnameable painful elation. A blurted sort of whoop, the holler of unstoppered belief. Because when the train lights hit the dimmest part of the billboard, a face appeared above the misty lake and it belonged to the murdered girl. A dozen women clutched their heads, they whooped and sobbed, a spirit, a godsbreath passing through the crowd.

Esmeralda.

Esmeralda.

Edgar was in body shock. She'd seen it but so fleetingly, too fast to absorb—she wanted the girl to reappear. Women holding babies up to the sign, to the flowing juice, let it bathe them in baptismal balsam and oil. And Sister Jan talking into Edgar's face, into the jangle of voices and noise.

"Did it look like her?"

"Yes."

"Are you sure?"

"I think so," Edgar said.

"Did you ever see her up close?"

"Neighborhood people have. Everyone here. They knew her for years."

Gracie would say, What a horror, what a spectacle of bad taste. She knew what Gracie would say. Gracie would say, It's just the undersheet, a technical flaw that causes an image from the papered-over ad to show through when sufficient light shines on the current ad.

Edgar saw Gracie clutching her throat, clawing theatrically for air.

Was she right? Had the news shed its dependence on the agencies that reported it? Was the news inventing itself on the eyeballs of walking talking people?

But what if there was no papered-over ad? Why should there be an ad under the orange juice ad? Surely they removed earlier ads.

Sister Jan said, "What now?"

They waited. They waited only eight or nine minutes this time before another train approached. Edgar moved, she tried to edge and gently elbow forward, and people made room, they saw her—a nun in a veil and long habit and winter cape followed by a sheepish helpmeet in a rummage coat and headscarf, holding aloft a portable phone.

They saw her and embraced her and she let them. Her presence was a verifying force, a figure from a universal church with sacraments and secret bank connections—she elects to follow a course of poverty, chastity and obedience. They embraced her and then let her pass and she was among the charismatic band, the gospelers rocking in place, when the train lamps swung their beams onto the billboard. She saw Esmeralda's face take shape under the rainbow of bounteous juice and above the little suburban lake and it had being and disposition, there was someone living in the image, a distinguishing spirit and character, the beauty of a reasoning creature—less than a second of life, less than half a second and the spot was dark again.

She felt something break upon her. She embraced Sister Jan. They shook hands, pumped hands with the great-bodied women who rolled their eyes to heaven. The women did great two-handed pump shakes, fabricated words jumping out of their mouths, trance utterance, Edgar thought—they're singing of things outside the known deliriums. She thumped a man's chest with her fists. Everything felt near at hand, breaking upon her, sadness and loss and glory and an old mother's bleak pity and a force at some deep level of lament that made her feel inseparable from the shakers and mourners, the awestruck who stood in tidal traffic—she was nameless for a moment, lost to the details of personal history, a disembodied fact in liquid form, pouring into the crowd.

Sister Jan said, "I don't know."

"Of course you know. You know. You saw her."

"I don't know. It was a shadow."

"Esmeralda on the lake."

"I don't know what I saw."

"You know. Of course you know. You saw her."

They waited for two more trains. Landing lights appeared in the sky and the planes kept dropping toward the runway across the water, another flight every half minute, the back-washed roars overlapping so everything was seamless noise and the air had a stink of smoky fuel. They waited for one more train.

How do things end, finally, things such as this—peter out to some forgotten core of weary faithful huddled in the rain?

The next night a thousand people filled the area. They parked their cars on the boulevard and tried to butt and pry their way onto the traffic island but most of them had to stand in the slow lane of the expressway, skittish and watchful. A woman was struck by a motorcycle, sent swirling into the asphalt. A boy was dragged a hundred yards, it is always a hundred yards, by a car that kept on going. Vendors moved along the lines of stalled traffic, selling flowers, soft drinks and live kittens. They sold laminated images of Esmeralda printed on prayer cards. They sold pinwheels that never stopped spinning.

The night after that the mother showed up, Esmeralda's lost mother, and she collapsed with flung arms when the girl's face appeared on the billboard. They took her away in an ambulance that was followed by a number of TV trucks. Two men fought with tire irons, blocking traffic on a ramp. Helicopter cameras filmed the scene and the police trailed orange caution tape through the area—the very orange of the living juice.

The next night the sign was blank. What a hole it made in space. People came and did not know what to say or think, where to look or what to believe. The sign was a white sheet with two microscopic words, SPACE AVAILABLE, followed by a phone number in tasteful type.

When the first train came, at dusk, the lights showed nothing.

And what do you remember, finally, when everyone has gone home and the streets are empty of devotion and hope, swept by river wind? Is the memory thin and bitter and does it shame you with its fundamental untruth—all nuance and wishful silhouette? Or does the power of transcendence linger, the sense of an event that violates natural forces, something holy that throbs on the hot horizon, the vision you crave because you need a sign to stand against your doubt?

Edgar held the image in her heart, the grained face on the lighted board, her virgin twin who was also her daughter. She recalled the smell of jet fuel. This became the incense of her experience, the burnt cedar and gum, a retaining medium that kept the moment whole, all the moments, the stunned raptures and swells of fellow feeling.

She felt the pain in her joints, the old body raw with routine pain, pain at the points of articulation, prods of sharp sensation in the links between bones.

She rose and prayed.

Pour forth we beseech Thee, O Lord, Thy grace into our hearts.

Ten years if recited at dawn, noon and eventide, or as soon thereafter as possible.

PART THREE

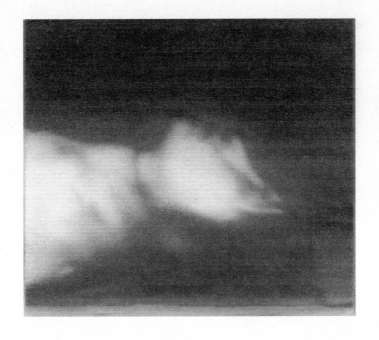

BAADER-MEINHOF

She knew there was someone else in the room. There was no outright noise, just an intimation behind her, a faint displacement of air. She'd been alone for a time, seated on a bench in the middle of the gallery with the paintings set around her, a cycle of fifteen canvases, and this is how it felt to her, that she was sitting as a person does in a mortuary chapel, keeping watch over the body of a relative or a friend.

This was sometimes called the viewing, she believed.

She was looking at Ulrike now, head and upper body, her neck rope-scorched, although she didn't know for certain what kind of implement had been used in the hanging.

She heard the other person walk toward the bench, a man's heavy shuffling stride, and she got up and went to stand before the picture of Ulrike, one of three related images, Ulrike dead in each, lying on the floor of her cell, head in profile. The canvases varied in size. The woman's reality, the head, the neck, the rope burn, the hair, the facial features, were painted, picture to picture, in nuances of obscurity and pall, a detail clearer here than there, the slurred mouth in one painting appearing nearly natural elsewhere, all of it unsystematic.

"Why do you think he did it this way?"

She did not turn to look at him.

"So shadowy. No color."

105

She said, "I don't know," and went to the next set of images, called *Man Shot Down*. This was Andreas Baader. She thought of him by his full name or surname. She thought of Meinhof, she saw Meinhof as first name only, Ulrike, and the same was the case with Gudrun.

"I'm trying to think what happened to them."

"They committed suicide. Or the state killed them."

He said, "The state." Then he said it again, deep-voiced, in a tone of melodramatic menace, trying out a line reading that might be more suitable.

She wanted to be annoyed but felt instead a vague cha-grin. It wasn't like her to use this term — *the state* — in the ironclad context of supreme public power. This was not her vocabulary.

The two paintings of Baader dead in his cell were the same size but addressed the subject somewhat differently, and this is what she did now — she concentrated on the differences, arm, shirt, unknown object at the edge of the frame, the disparity or uncertainty.

"I don't know what happened," she said. "I'm only telling you what people believe. It was twenty-five years ago. I don't know what it was like then, in Germany, with bombings and kidnappings."

"They made an agreement, don't you think?"

"Some people believe they were murdered in their cells."

"A pact. They were terrorists, weren't they? When they're not killing other people, they're killing themselves," he said.

She was looking at Andreas Baader, first one painting, then the other, then back again.

"I don't know. Maybe that's even worse in a way. It's so much sadder. There's so much sadness in these pictures."

"There's one that's smiling," he said.

This was Gudrun, in *Confrontation 2*.

"I don't know if that's a smile. It could be a smile."

"It's the clearest image in the room. Maybe the whole museum. She's smiling," he said.

She turned to look at Gudrun across the gallery and saw the man on the bench, half turned her way, wearing a suit with tie unknotted, going prematurely bald. She only glimpsed him. He was looking at her but she was looking past him to the figure of Gudrun in a prison smock, standing against a wall and smiling, most likely, yes, in the middle picture. Three paintings of Gudrun, maybe smiling, smiling and probably not smiling.

"You need special training to look at these pictures. I can't tell the people apart."

"Yes, you can. Just look. You have to look."

She heard a note of slight reprimand in her voice. She went to the far wall to look at the painting of one of the jail cells, with tall bookshelves covering nearly half the canvas and a dark shape, wraithlike, that may have been a coat on a hanger.

"You're a grad student. Or you teach art," he said. "I'm frankly here to pass the time. That's what I do between job interviews."

She didn't want to tell him that she'd been here three straight days. She moved to the adjacent wall, a little closer to his position on the bench. Then she told him.

"Major money," he said. "Unless you're a member."

"I'm not a member."

"Then you teach art."

"I don't teach art."

"You want me to shut up. Shut up, Bob. Only my name's not Bob."

In the painting of the coffins being carried through a large crowd, she didn't know they were coffins at first. It took her a long moment to see the crowd itself. There was the crowd, mostly an ashy blur with a few figures in the center-right foreground discernible as individuals standing with their backs to the viewer, and then there was a break near the top of the canvas, a pale strip of earth or roadway, and then another mass of people or trees, and it took some time to understand that the three whitish objects near the center of the picture were coffins being carried through the crowd or simply propped on biers.

Here were the bodies of Andreas Baader, Gudrun Ensslin and a man whose name she could not recall. He had been shot in his cell. Baader had also been shot. Gudrun had been hanged.

She knew that this had happened about a year and a half after Ulrike. Ulrike dead in May, she knew, of 1976.

Two men entered the gallery, followed by a woman with a cane. All three stood before the display of explanatory material, reading.

The painting of the coffins had something else that wasn't easy to find. She hadn't found it until the second day, yesterday, and it was striking once she'd found it, and inescapable now—an object at the top of the painting, just left of center, a tree perhaps, in the rough shape of a cross.

She went closer to the painting, hearing the woman with the cane move toward the opposite wall.

She knew that these paintings were based on photographs but she hadn't seen them and didn't know whether there was

BAADER-MEINHOF

a bare tree, a dead tree beyond the cemetery, in one of the photos, that consisted of a spindly trunk with a single branch remaining, or two branches forming a transverse piece near the top of the trunk.

He was standing next to her now, the man she'd been talking to.

"Tell me what you see. Honestly, I want to know."

A group entered, led by a guide, and she turned for a moment, watching them collect at the first painting in the cycle, the portrait of Ulrike as a much younger woman, a girl, really, distant and wistful, her hand and face half floating in the somber dark around her.

"I realize now that the first day I was only barely looking. I thought I was looking but I was only getting a bare inkling of what's in these paintings. I'm only just starting to look."

They stood looking, together, at the coffins and trees and crowd. The tour guide began speaking to her group.

"And what do you feel when you look?" he said.

"I don't know. It's complicated."

"Because I don't feel anything."

"I think I feel helpless. These paintings make me feel how helpless a person can be."

"Is that why you're here three straight days? To feel helpless?" he said.

"I'm here because I love the paintings. More and more. At first I was confused, and still am, a little. But I know I love the paintings now."

It was a cross. She saw it as a cross and it made her feel, right or wrong, that there was an element of forgiveness in the picture, that the two men and the woman, terrorists, and Ulrike before them, terrorist, were not beyond forgiveness.

109

But she didn't point out the cross to the man standing next to her. That was not what she wanted, a discussion on the subject. She didn't think she was imagining a cross, seeing a cross in some free strokes of paint, but she didn't want to hear someone raise elementary doubts.

They went to a snack bar and sat on stools arranged along a narrow counter that measured the length of the front window. She watched the crowds on Seventh Avenue, half the world rushing by, and barely tasted what she ate.

"I missed the first-day pop," he said, "where the stock soars like mythically, four hundred percent in a couple of hours. I got there for the aftermarket, which turned out to be weak, then weaker."

When the stools were all occupied, people stood and ate. She wanted to go home and check her phone messages.

"I make appointments now. I shave, I smile. My life is living hell," he said, blandly, chewing as he spoke.

He took up space, a tall broad man with a looseness about him, something offhand and shambling. Someone reached past her to snag a napkin from the dispenser. She had no idea what she was doing here, talking to this man.

He said, "No color. No meaning."

"What they did had meaning. It was wrong but it wasn't blind and empty. I think the painter's searching for this. And how did it end the way it did? I think he's asking this. Everybody dead."

"How else could it end? Tell the truth," he said. "You teach art to handicapped children."

She didn't know whether this was interesting or cruel but saw herself in the window wearing a grudging smile.

"I don't teach art."

"This is fast food that I'm trying to eat slow. I don't have an appointment until three-thirty. Eat slow. And tell me what you teach."

"I don't teach."

She didn't tell him that she was also out of work. She'd grown tired of describing her job, administrative, with an educational publisher, so why make the effort, she thought, now that the job and the company no longer existed.

"Problem is, it's against my nature to eat slow. I have to remind myself. But even then I can't make the adjustment."

But that wasn't the reason. She didn't tell him that she was out of work because it would give them a situation in common. She didn't want that, an inflection of mutual sympathy, a comradeship. Let the tone stay scattered.

She drank her apple juice and looked at the crowds moving past, at faces that seemed completely knowable for half a second or so, then were forgotten forever in far less time than that.

He said, "We should have gone to a real restaurant. It's hard to talk here. You're not comfortable."

"No, this is fine. I'm kind of in a rush right now."

He seemed to consider this and then reject it, undiscouraged. She thought of going to the washroom and then thought no. She thought of the dead man's shirt, Andreas Baader's shirt, dirtier or more bloody in one picture than in the other.

"And you have a three o'clock," she said.

"Three-thirty. But that's a long way off. That's another world, where I fix my tie and walk in and tell them who I am." He paused a moment, then looked at her. "You're supposed to say, 'Who are you?'"

111

She saw herself smile. But she said nothing. She thought that maybe Ulrike's rope burn wasn't a burn but the rope itself, if it was a rope and not a wire or a belt or something else.

He said, "That's your line. 'Who are you?' I set you up beautifully and you totally miss your cue."

They'd finished eating but their paper cups were not empty yet. They talked about rents and leases, parts of town. She didn't want to tell him where she lived. She lived just three blocks away, in a faded brick building whose limitations and malfunctions she'd come to understand as the texture of her life, to be distinguished from a normal day's complaints.

Then she told him. They were talking about places to run and bike, and he told her where he lived and what his jogging route was, and she said that her bike had been stolen from the basement of her building, and when he asked her where she lived she told him, more or less nonchalantly, and he drank his diet soda and looked out the window, or into it, perhaps, at their faint reflections paired on the glass.

When she came out of the bathroom, he was standing at the kitchen window as if waiting for a view to materialize. There was nothing out there but dusty masonry and glass, the rear of the industrial loft building on the next street.

It was a studio apartment, with the kitchen only partly walled off and the bed in a corner of the room, smallish, without posts or headboard, covered in a bright Berber robe, the only object in the room of some slight distinction.

She knew she had to offer him a drink. She felt awkward, unskilled at this, at unexpected guests. Where to sit, what to say, these were matters to consider. She didn't mention the gin she kept in the freezer.

"You've lived here, what?"

"Just under four months. I've been a nomad," she said. "Sublets, staying with friends, always short-term. Ever since the marriage failed."

"The marriage."

He said this in a modified version of the baritone rumble he'd used earlier for "the state."

"I've never been married. Believe that?" he said. "Most of my friends my age. All of them really. Married, children, divorced, children. You want kids someday?"

"When is someday? Yes, I think so."

"I think of kids. It makes me feel selfish, to be so wary of having a family. Never mind do I have a job or not. I'll have a job soon, a good one. That's not it. I'm in awe of raising, basically, someone so tiny and soft."

They drank seltzer with wedges of lemon, seated diagonally at the low wooden table, the coffee table where she ate her meals. The conversation surprised her a little. It was not difficult, even in the pauses. The pauses were unembarrassed and he seemed honest in his remarks.

His cell phone rang. He dug it out of his body and spoke briefly, then sat with the thing in his hand, looking thoughtful.

"I should remember to turn it off. But I think, If I turn it off, what will I miss? Something so incredible."

"The call that changes everything."

"Something so incredible. The total life-altering call. That's why I respect my cell phone."

She wanted to look at the clock.

"That wasn't your interview just now, was it? Canceled?"

He said it wasn't and she sneaked a look at the clock on the wall. She wondered whether she wanted him to miss his interview. That couldn't be what she wanted.

"Maybe you're like me," he said. "You have to find yourself on the verge of something happening before you can begin to prepare for it. That's when you get serious."

"Are we talking about fatherhood?"

"Actually, I canceled the interview myself. When you were in there," he said, nodding toward the bathroom.

She felt an odd panic. He finished his seltzer, tipping his head back until an ice cube slid into his mouth. They sat awhile, letting the ice melt. Then he looked directly at her, fingering one of the dangled ends of his necktie.

"Tell me what you want."

She sat there.

"Because I sense you're not ready and I don't want to do something too soon. But, you know, we're here."

She didn't look at him.

"I'm not one of those controlling men. I don't need to control anyone. Tell me what you want."

"Nothing."

"Conversation, talk, whatever. Affection," he said. "This is not a major moment in the world. It'll come and go. But we're here, so."

"I want you to leave, please."

He shrugged and said, "Whatever." Then he sat there.

"You said, 'Tell me what you want.' I want you to leave."

He sat there. He didn't move. He said, "I canceled the thing for a reason. I don't think this is the reason, this particular conversation. I'm looking at you. I'm saying to myself, You know what she's like? She's like someone convalescing."

"I'm willing to say it was my mistake."

"I mean we're here. How did this happen? There was no mistake. Let's be friends," he said.

"I think we have to stop now."

"Stop what? What are we doing?"

He was trying to speak softly, to take the edge off the moment.

"She's like someone convalescing. Even in the museum, this is what I thought. All right. Fine. But now we're here. This whole day, no matter what we say or do, it'll come and go."

"I don't want to continue this."

"Be friends."

"This is not right."

"No, be friends."

His voice carried an intimacy so false it seemed a little threatening. She didn't know why she was still sitting here. He leaned toward her then, placing a hand lightly on her forearm.

"I don't try to control people. This is not me."

She drew away and stood up and he was all around her then. She tucked her head into her shoulder. He didn't exert pressure or try to caress her breasts or hips but held her in a kind of loose containment. For a moment she seemed to disappear, tucked and still, in breathless hiding. Then she pulled away. He let her do this and looked at her so levelly, with such measuring effect, that she barely recognized him. He was ranking her, marking her in some awful and withering way.

"Be friends," he said.

She found she was shaking her head, trying to disbelieve

the moment, to make it reversible, a misunderstanding. He watched her. She was standing near the bed and this was precisely the information contained in his look, these two things, her and the bed. He shrugged as if to say, It's only right. Because what's the point of being here if we don't do what we're here to do? Then he took off his jacket, a set of unhurried movements that seemed to use up the room. In the rumpled white shirt he was bigger than ever, sweating, completely unknown to her. He held the jacket at his side, arm extended.

"See how easy. Now you. Start with the shoes," he said. "First one, then the other."

She went toward the bathroom. She didn't know what to do. She walked along the wall, head down, a person marching blindly, and went into the bathroom. She closed the door but was afraid to lock it. She thought it would make him angry, provoke him to do something, wreck something, worse. She did not slide the bolt. She was determined not to do this unless she heard him approach the bathroom. She didn't think he'd moved. She was certain, nearly certain that he was standing near the coffee table.

She said, "Please leave."

Her voice was unnatural, so fluted and small it scared her further. Then she heard him move. It sounded almost leisurely. It was a saunter, almost, and it took him past the radiator, where the cover rattled slightly, and in the direction of the bed.

"You have to go," she said, louder now.

He was sitting on the bed, unbuckling his belt. This is what she thought she heard, the tip of the belt sliding out of the loop and then a little flick of tongue and clasp. She heard the zipper coming down.

She stood against the bathroom door. After a while she heard him breathing, a sound of concentrated work, nasal and cadenced. She stood there and waited, head down, body on the door. There was nothing she could do but listen and wait.

When he was finished, there was a long pause, then some rustling and shifting. She thought she heard him put on his jacket. He came toward her now. She realized she could have locked the door earlier, when he was on the bed. She stood there and waited. Then she felt him lean against the door, the dead weight of him, an inch away, not pushing but sagging. She slid the bolt into the chamber, quietly. He was pressed there, breathing, sinking into the door.

He said, "Forgive me."

His voice was barely audible, close to a moan. She stood there, and waited.

He said, "I'm so sorry. Please. I don't know what to say."

She waited for him to leave. When she heard him cross the room and close the door behind him, finally, she waited a full minute longer. Then she came out of the bathroom and locked the front door.

She saw everything twice now. She was where she wanted to be, and alone, but nothing was the same. Bastard. Nearly everything in the room had a double effect—what it was and the association it carried in her mind. She went out walking and when she came back the connection was still there, at the coffee table, on the bed, in the bathroom. Bastard. She had dinner in a small restaurant nearby and went to bed early.

*   *   *

When she went back to the museum the next morning he was alone in the gallery, seated on the bench in the middle of the room, his back to the entranceway, and he was looking at the last painting in the cycle, the largest by far and maybe most breathtaking, the one with the coffins and cross, called *Funeral*.

MIDNIGHT IN
DOSTOEVSKY

We were two somber boys hunched in our coats, grim winter settling in. The college was at the edge of a small town way upstate, barely a town, maybe a hamlet, we said, or just a whistle-stop, and we took walks all the time, getting out, going nowhere, low skies and bare trees, hardly a soul to be seen. This was how we spoke of the local people: they were souls, they were transient spirits, a face in the window of a passing car, runny with reflected light, or a long street with a shovel jutting from a snowbank, no one in sight.

We were walking parallel to the tracks when an old freight train approached and we stopped and watched. It seemed the kind of history that passes mostly unobserved, a diesel engine and a hundred boxcars rolling over remote country, and we shared an unspoken moment of respect, Todd and I, for times past, frontiers gone, and then walked on, talking about nothing much but making something of it. We heard the whistle sound as the train disappeared into late afternoon.

This was the day we saw the man in the hooded coat. We argued about the coat—loden coat, anorak, parka. It was our routine; we were ever ready to find a matter to contest.

This was why the man had been born, to end up in this town wearing that coat. He was well ahead of us and walking slowly, hands clasped behind his back, a smallish figure turning now to enter a residential street and fade from view.

"A loden coat doesn't have a hood. A hood isn't part of the context," Todd said. "It's a parka or an anorak."

"There's others. There's always others."

"Name one."

"Duffel coat."

"There's duffel bag."

"There's duffel coat."

"Does the word imply a hood?"

"The word implies toggles."

"The coat had a hood. We don't know if the coat had toggles."

"Doesn't matter," I said. "Because the guy was wearing a parka."

"*Anorak* is an Inuit word."

"So what."

"I say it's an anorak," he said.

I tried to invent an etymology for the word *parka* but couldn't think fast enough. Todd was on another subject— the freight train, laws of motion, effects of force, sneaking in a question about the number of boxcars that trailed the locomotive. We hadn't stated in advance that a tally would be taken, but each of us had known that the other would be counting, even as we spoke about other things. When I told him now what my number was, he did not respond, and I knew what this meant. It meant that he'd arrived at the same number. This was not supposed to happen—it unsettled us, it made the world flat—and we walked for a time in chagrined silence. Even in matters of pure physical reality, we depended on a friction between our basic faculties of sensation, his and mine, and we understood now that the rest of the afternoon would be spent in the marking of differences.

We headed back for a late class.

"An anorak is substantial. The thing he was wearing looked pretty flimsy," I said. "And an anorak would have a fur-lined hood. Consider the origin of the word. You're the one who brought up the Inuits. Wouldn't an Inuit use fur to line his hood? They have polar bear. They have walrus. They need coats with bulk and substance top to bottom."

"We saw the guy from behind," he said. "How do you know what kind of hood it was? From behind and from a distance."

Consider the origin of the word. I was using his Inuit lore against him, forcing him to respond reasonably, a rare sign of weakness on his part. Todd was a determined thinker who liked to work a fact or an idea to the seventh level of interpretation. He was tall and sprawling, all bony framework, the kind of body not always in sync with its hinges and joints. Somebody said that he resembled the love child of storks, others thought ostriches. He did not seem to taste food; he consumed it, absorbed it, ingestible matter of plant or animal origin. He spoke of distances in meters and kilometers and it took me a while to understand that this was not an affectation so much as a driving need to convert units of measurement more or less instantaneously. He liked to test himself on what he knew. He liked to stop walking to emphasize a point as I walked on. This was my counterpoint, to let him stand there talking to a tree. The shallower our arguments, the more intense we became.

I wanted to keep this one going, to stay in control, to press him hard. Did it matter what I said?

"Even from a distance the hood looked too small to be fur-lined. The hood was snug," I said. "A true anorak would have a hood that's roomy enough to fit a woolen cap underneath. Isn't that what the Inuits do?"

The campus appeared in fragments through ranks of tall trees on the other side of a country road. We lived in a series of energy-efficient structures with solar panels, turfed rooftops and red cedar walls. Classes were held in the original buildings, several massive concrete units known collectively as the Cellblock, a bike ride or long walk away from the dorms, and the flow of students back and forth in tribal swarms seemed part of the architecture of the place. This was my first year here and I was still trying to interpret the signs and adapt to the patterns.

"They have caribou," I said. "They have seal meat and ice floes."

At times abandon meaning to impulse. Let the words be the facts. This was the nature of our walks — to register what was out there, all the scattered rhythms of circumstance and occurrence, and to reconstruct it as human noise.

The class was Logic, in Cellblock 2, thirteen of us seated along both sides of a long table, with Ilgauskas at the head, a stocky man, late forties, beset this day by periodic coughing. He spoke from a standing position, bent forward, hands set on the table, and often stared for long moments into the blank wall at the other end of the room.

"The causal nexus," he said, and stared into the wall.

He stared, we glanced. We exchanged glances frequently,

one side of the table with the other. We were fascinated by Ilgauskas. He seemed a man in a trance state. But he wasn't simply absent from his remarks, another drained voice echoing down the tunnel of teaching years. We'd decided, some of us, that he was suffering from a neurological condition. He was not bored but simply unbound, speaking freely and erratically out of a kind of stricken insight. It was a question of neurochemistry. We'd decided that the condition was not understood well enough to have been given a name. And if it did not have a name, we said, paraphrasing a proposition in logic, then it could not be treated.

"The atomic fact," he said.

Then he elaborated for ten minutes while we listened, glanced, made notes, riffled the textbook to find refuge in print, some semblance of meaning that might be roughly equivalent to what he was saying. There were no laptops or handheld devices in class. Ilgauskas didn't exclude them; we did, sort of, unspokenly. Some of us could barely complete a thought without touch pads or scroll buttons but we understood that high-speed data systems did not belong here. They were an assault on the environment, which was defined by length, width and depth, with time drawn out, computed in heartbeats. We sat and listened or sat and waited. We wrote with pens or pencils. Our notebooks had pages made of flexible sheets of paper.

I tried to exchange glances with the girl across the table. This was the first time we'd been seated face to face but she kept looking down at her notes, her hands, maybe the grain of the wood along the edge of the table. I told myself that she was averting her eyes not from me but from Ilgauskas.

"F and not-F," he said.

He made her shy, the blunt impact of the man, thick body, strong voice, staccato cough, even the old dark suit he wore, unpressed, to every class, his chest hair curling up out of the open shirt collar. He used German and Latin terms without defining them. I tried to insert myself into the girl's line of sight, scrunching down and peering up. We listened earnestly, all of us, hoping to understand and to transcend the need to understand.

Sometimes he coughed into his cupped hand, other times into the table, and we imagined microscopic life-forms teeming toward the tabletop and ricocheting into breathable space. Those seated nearest him ducked away with a wince that was also a smile, half apologetic. The shy girl's shoulders quivered, even though she was sitting at some distance from the man. We didn't expect Ilgauskas to excuse himself. He was Ilgauskas. We were the ones at fault, for being there to witness the coughing, or for not being adequate to the seismic scale of it, or for other reasons not yet known to us.

"Can we ask this question?" he said.

We waited for the question. We wondered whether the question he'd asked was the question we were waiting for him to ask. In other words, could he ask the question he was asking? It was not a trick, not a game or a logical puzzle. Ilgauskas didn't do that. We sat and waited. He stared into the wall at the far end of the room.

It felt good to be out in the weather, that wintry sting of approaching snow. I was walking down a street of older houses, some in serious need of repair, sad and handsome, bay window here, curved porch there, when he turned the corner and came toward me, slightly crouched, same coat, face nearly lost inside the hood. He was walking slowly, as before, hands behind his back, as before, and he seemed to pause when he saw me, almost imperceptibly, head lowered now, path not quite steady.

There was no one else on the street. As we approached each other, he veered away, and then so did I, just slightly, to reassure him, but I also sent a stealthy look his way. The face inside the hood was stubbled—gray old man, I thought, large nose, eyes on the sidewalk but also noting my presence. After we'd passed each other I waited a moment and then turned and looked. He wasn't wearing gloves and this seemed fitting, I'm not sure why, no gloves, despite the unrelenting cold.

About an hour later, I was part of the mass movement of students going in opposite directions, in wind-whipped snow, two roughly parallel columns moving from old campus to new and vice versa, faces in ski masks, bodies shouldering into the wind or pushed along by it. I saw Todd, long-striding, and pointed. This was our standard sign of greeting or approval—we pointed. I shouted into the weather as he went by.

"Saw him again. Same coat, same hood, different street."

He nodded and pointed back and two days later we were walking in the outlying parts of town. I gestured toward a pair of large trees, bare branches forking up fifty or sixty feet.

"Norway maple," I said.

He said nothing. They meant nothing to him, trees, birds, baseball teams. He knew music, classical to serial, and the history of mathematics, and a hundred other things. I knew trees from summer camp, when I was twelve, and I was

pretty sure the trees were maples. Norway was another matter. I could have said red maple or sugar maple but Norway
sounded stronger, more informed.

We both played chess. We both believed in God.

Houses here loomed over the street and we saw a middle-
aged woman get out of her car and take a baby stroller from
the rear seat and unfold it. Then she took four grocery bags
from the car, one at a time, and placed each in the stroller.
We were talking and watching. We were talking about epi-
demics, pandemics and plagues, but we were watching the
woman. She shut the car door and pulled the stroller backward over the hard-packed snow on the sidewalk and up the
long flight of steps to her porch.

"What's her name?"

"Isabel," I said.

"Be serious. We're serious people. What's her name?"

"Okay, what's her name?"

"Her name is Mary Frances. Listen to me," he whispered.
"*Mar-y Fran-ces.* Never just Mary."

"Okay, maybe."

"Where the hell do you get Isabel?"

He showed mock concern, placing a hand on my shoulder.

"I don't know. Isabel's her sister. They're identical twins.
Isabel's the alcoholic twin. But you're missing the central
questions."

"No, I'm not. Where's the baby that goes with the stroller?
Whose baby is it?" he said. "What's the baby's name?"

We started down the street that led out of town and heard
aircraft from the military base. I turned and looked up and
they were there and gone, three fighter jets wheeling to
the east, and then I saw the hooded man a hundred yards

away, coming over the crest of a steep street, headed in our direction.

I said, "Don't look now."

Todd turned and looked. I talked him into crossing the street to put some space between the man and us. We watched from a driveway, standing under a weathered backboard and rim fastened to the ridge beam above the garage door. A pickup went by and the man stopped briefly, then walked on.

"See the coat. No toggles," I said.

"Because it's an anorak."

"It's a parka—it was always a parka. Hard to tell from here but I think he shaved. Or someone shaved him. Whoever he lives with. A son or daughter, grandkids."

He was directly across the street from us now, moving cautiously to avoid stretches of unshoveled snow.

"He's not from here," Todd said. "He's from somewhere in Europe. They brought him over. He couldn't take care of himself anymore. His wife died. They wanted to stay where they were, the two elderly people. But then she died."

He was speaking distantly, Todd was, watching the man but talking through him, finding his shadow somewhere on the other side of the world. The man did not see us, I was sure of this. He reached the corner, one of his hands behind his back, the other making small conversational gestures, and then he turned onto the next street and was gone.

"Did you see his shoes?"

"They weren't boots."

"They were shoes that reach to the ankle."

"High shoes."

"Old World."

"No gloves."

"Jacket below the knees."

"Possibly not his."

"A hand-me-down or hand-me-up."

"Think of the hat he'd be wearing if he was wearing a hat," I said.

"He's not wearing a hat."

"But if he was wearing a hat, what kind of hat?"

"He's wearing a hood."

"But what kind of hat, if he was wearing a hat?"

"He's wearing a hood," Todd said.

We walked down to the corner now and started across the street. He spoke an instant before I did.

"There's only one kind of hat he could conceivably wear. A hat with an earflap that reaches from one ear around the back of the head to the other ear. An old soiled cap. A peaked cap with a flap for the ears."

I said nothing. I had nothing to say to this.

There was no sign of the man along the street he'd entered. For a couple of seconds an aura of mystery hovered over the scene. But his disappearance simply meant that he lived in one of the houses on the street. Did it matter which house? I didn't think it mattered but Todd disagreed. He wanted a house that matched the man.

We walked slowly down the middle of the street, six feet apart, using rutted car tracks in the snow to make the going easier. He took off a glove and extended his hand, fingers spread and flexing.

"Feel the air. I say minus nine Celsius."

"We're not Celsius."

"But he is, where he's from, that's Celsius."

"Where *is* he from? There's something not too totally white about him. He's not Scandinavian."

"Not Dutch or Irish."

I wondered about Andalusian. Where was Andalusia exactly? I didn't think I knew. Or an Uzbek, a Kazakh. But these seemed irresponsible.

"Middle Europe," Todd said. "Eastern Europe."

He pointed to a gray frame house, an ordinary two-story, with a shingled roof and no sign of the fallen grace that defined some of the houses elsewhere in town.

"Could be that one. His family allows him to take a walk now and then, provided he stays within a limited area."

"The cold doesn't bother him much."

"He's used to colder."

"Plus, he has very little feeling in his extremities," I said.

There was no Christmas wreath on the front door, no holiday lights. I didn't see anything about the property that might suggest who lived there, from what background, speaking which language. We approached the point where the street ended in a patch of woods, and we turned and headed back.

We had class in half an hour and I wanted to speed up the pace. Todd was still looking at houses. I thought of the Baltic states and the Balkan states, briefly confused — which was which and which was where.

I spoke before he did.

"I see him as a figure who escaped the war in the 1990s. Croatia, Serbia, Bosnia. Or who didn't leave until recently."

"I don't feel that here," he said. "It's not the right model."

"Or he's Greek, and his name is Spyros."

"I wish you a painless death," he said, not bothering to look my way.

"German names. Names with umlauts."

This last had nothing but nuisance value. I knew that. I tried walking faster but he paused a moment, standing in his skewed way to look at the gray house.

"In a few hours, think of it, dinner's over, the others are watching TV, he's in his little room sitting on the edge of a narrow bed in his long johns, staring into space."

I wondered if this was a space that Todd expected us to fill.

We waited through the long silences and then nodded when he coughed, in collegial approval. He'd coughed only twice so far today. There was a small puckered bandage at the edge of his jaw. He shaves, we thought. He cuts himself and says *shit*. He wads up a sheet of toilet paper and holds it to the cut. Then he leans into the mirror, seeing himself clearly for the first time in years.

Ilgauskas, he thinks.

We never took the same seats, class after class. We weren't sure how this had started. One of us, in a spirit of offhand mischief, may have spread the word that Ilgauskas preferred it this way. In fact the idea had substance. He didn't want to know who we were. We were passersby to him, smeary faces, we were roadkill. It was an aspect of his neurological condition, we thought, to regard others as displaceable, and this seemed interesting, seemed part of the course, displaceability, one of the truth functions that he referred to now and then.

But we were violating the code, the shy girl and I, seated face to face once again. This happened because I had entered the room after she did and had simply fallen into the empty chair directly across from her. She knew I was there, knew it was me, same gaping lad, eager to make eye contact.

"Imagine a surface of no color whatsoever," he said.

We sat there and imagined. He ran a hand through his dark hair, a shaggy mass that flopped in several directions. He did not bring books to class, never a sign of the textbook or a sheaf of notes, and his shambling discourses made us feel that we were becoming what he saw before him, an amorphous entity. We were basically stateless. He could have been speaking to political prisoners in orange jumpsuits. We admired this. We were in the Cellblock, after all. We exchanged glances, she and I, tentatively. Ilgauskas leaned toward the table, eyes swimming with neurochemical life. He looked at the wall, talked to the wall.

"Logic ends where the world ends," he said.

The world, yes. But he seemed to be speaking with his back to the world. Then again the subject was not history or geography. He was instructing us in the principles of pure reason. We listened intently. One remark dissolved into the next. He was an artist, an abstract artist. He asked a series of questions and we made earnest notes. The questions he asked were unanswerable, at least by us, and he was not expecting answers in any case. We did not speak in class; no one ever spoke. There were never any questions, student to professor. That steadfast tradition was dead here.

He said, "Facts, pictures, things."

What did he mean by "things"? We would probably never know. Were we too passive, too accepting of the man? Did we see dysfunction and call it an inspired form of intellect? We didn't want to like him, only to believe in him. We tendered our deepest trust to the stark nature of his methodology. Of course there was no methodology. There was only Ilgauskas. He challenged our reason for being, what we thought, how we lived, the truth or falsity of what we believed to be true or false. Isn't this what great teachers do, the Zen masters and Brahman scholars?

He leaned toward the table and spoke about meanings fixed in advance. We listened hard and tried to understand. But to understand at this point in our study, months along, would have been confusing, even a kind of disillusionment. He said something in Latin, hands pressed flat to the table-top, and then he did a strange thing. He looked at us, eyes gliding up one row of faces, down the other. We were all there, we were always there, our usual shrouded selves. Finally he raised his hand and looked at his watch. It didn't matter what time it was. The gesture itself meant that class was over.

A meaning fixed in advance, we thought.

We sat there, she and I, while the others gathered books and papers and lifted coats off chair backs. She was pale and thin, hair pinned back, and I had an idea that she wanted to look neutral, seem neutral in order to challenge people to notice her. She placed her textbook on top of her notebook, centering it precisely, then raised her head and waited for me to say something.

"Okay, what's your name?"

"Jenna. What's yours?"

"I want to say Lars-Magnus just to see if you believe me."

"I don't."

"It's Robby," I said.

"I saw you working out in the fitness center."

"I was on the elliptical. Where were you?"

"Just passing by, I guess."

"Is that what you do?"

"Pretty much all the time," she said.

The last to leave were shuffling out now. She stood and dropped her books into her backpack, which dangled from the chair. I remained where I was, watching.

"I'm curious to know what you have to say about this man."

"The professor."

"Do you have insights to offer?"

"I talked to him once," she said. "Person to person."

"Are you serious? Where?"

"At the diner in town."

"You talked to him?"

"I get off-campus urges. I have to go somewhere."

"I know the feeling."

"It's the only place to eat, other than here, so I walked in and sat down and there he was in the booth across the aisle."

"That's incredible."

"I sat there and thought, It's him."

"It's him."

"There was a big foldout menu that I hid behind while I kept sneaking looks. He was eating a full meal, something slopped in brown gravy from the center of the earth. And he had a Coke with a straw bending out of the can."

"You talked to him."

"I said something not too original and we talked off and on. He had his coat thrown onto the seat opposite him and I was eating a salad and there was a book lying on top of his coat and I asked him what he was reading."

"You talked to him. The man who makes you lower your eyes in primitive fear and dread."

"It was a diner. He was drinking Coke through a straw," she said.

"Fantastic. What was he reading?"

"He said he was reading Dostoevsky. I'll tell you exactly what he said. He said, 'Dostoevsky day and night.'"

"Fantastic."

"And I told him my coincidence, that I'd been reading a lot of poetry and I'd read a poem just a couple of days earlier with a phrase I recalled. 'Like midnight in Dostoevsky.'"

"What did he say?"

"Nothing."

"Does he read Dostoevsky in the original?"

"I didn't ask."

"I wonder if he does. I have a feeling he does."

There was a pause and then she said that she was leaving school. I was thinking about Ilgauskas in the diner. She told me that she wasn't happy here, that her mother always said how accomplished she was at being unhappy. She was heading west, she said, to Idaho. I didn't say anything. I sat there with my hands folded at my belt line. She left without a coat. Her coat was probably in the coatrack on the first floor.

At the winter break I stayed on campus, one of the few. We called ourselves The Left Behind and spoke in broken English. The routine included zombie body posture and blurred vision, lasting half a day before we'd all had enough.

At the gym I did my dumb struts on the elliptical and lapsed into spells of lost thought. Idaho, I thought. Idaho, the word, so voweled and obscure. Wasn't where we were, right here, obscure enough for her?

The library was deserted during the break. I entered with

a keycard and took a novel by Dostoevsky down from the shelves. I placed the book on a table and opened it and then leaned down into the splayed pages, reading and breathing. We seemed to assimilate each other, the characters and I, and when I raised my head I had to tell myself where I was.

I knew where my father was — in Beijing, trying to wedge his securities firm into the Chinese century. My mother was adrift, possibly in the Florida Keys with a former boyfriend named Raúl. My father pronounced it *raw-eel*, like a thing you eat with your eyes closed.

In snowfall, the town looked ghosted over, dead still at times. I took walks nearly every afternoon and the man in the hooded coat was never far from my mind. I walked up and down the street where he lived and it seemed only fitting that he was not to be seen. This was an essential quality of the place. I began to feel intimate with these streets. I was myself here, able to see things singly and plainly, away from the only life I'd known, the city, stacked and layered, a thousand meanings a minute.

On the stunted commercial street in town there were three places still open for business, one of them the diner, and I ate there once and stuck my head in the door two or three times, scanning the booths. The sidewalk was old pocked bluestone. In the convenience store I bought a fudge bar and talked to the woman behind the counter about her son's wife's kidney infection.

At the library I devoured about a hundred pages a sitting, small cramped type. When I left the building the book remained on the table, open to the page where I'd stopped reading. I returned the next day and the book was still there, open to the same page.

Why did this seem magical? Why did I sometimes lie in bed, moments from sleep, and think of the book in the empty room, open to the page where I'd stopped reading?

On one of those midnights, just before classes resumed, I got out of bed and went down the hall to the sun parlor. The area was enclosed by a slanted canopy of partitioned glass and I unlatched a panel and swung it open. My pajamas seemed to evaporate. I felt the cold in my pores, my teeth. I thought my teeth were ringing. I stood and looked, I was always looking. I felt childlike now, responding to a dare. How long could I take it? I peered into the northern sky, the living sky, my breath turning to little bursts of smoke as if I were separating from my body. I'd come to love the cold but this was idiotic and I closed the panel and went back to my room. I paced awhile, swinging my arms across my chest, trying to roil the blood, warm the body, and twenty minutes after I was back in bed, wide awake, the idea came to mind. It came from nowhere, from the night, fully formed, extending in several directions, and when I opened my eyes in the morning it was all around me, filling the room.

Those afternoons the light died quickly and we talked nearly nonstop, race-walking into the wind. Every topic had spectral connections, Todd's congenital liver condition shading into my ambition to run a marathon, this leading to that, the theory of prime numbers to the living sight of rural mailboxes set along a lost road, eleven standing units, rusted over and near collapse, a prime number, Todd announced, using his cell phone to take a picture.

One day we approached the street where the hooded man lived. This was when I told Todd about the idea I'd had, the revelation in the icy night. I knew who the man was, I said. Everything fit, every element, the man's origins, his family ties, his presence in this town.

He said, "Okay."

"First, he's a Russian."

"A Russian."

"He's here because his son is here."

"He doesn't have the bearing of a Russian."

"The bearing? What's the bearing? His name could easily be Pavel."

"No, it couldn't."

"Great name possibilities. Pavel, Mikhail, Aleksei. Viktor with a *k*. His late wife was Tatiana."

We stopped and looked down the street toward the gray frame house designated as the place where the man lived.

"Listen to me," I said. "His son lives in this town because he teaches at the college. His name is Ilgauskas."

I waited for him to be stunned.

"Ilgauskas is the son of the man in the hooded coat," I said. "Our Ilgauskas. They're Russian, father and son."

I pointed at him and waited for him to point back.

He said, "Ilgauskas is too old to be the man's son."

"He's not even fifty. The man is in his seventies, easy. Mid-seventies, most likely. It fits, it works."

"Is Ilgauskas a Russian name?"

"Why wouldn't it be?"

"Somewhere else, somewhere nearby, but not necessarily Russian," he said.

We stood there looking toward the house. I should have anticipated this kind of resistance but the idea had been so striking that it overwhelmed my cautious instincts.

"There's something you don't know about Ilgauskas."

He said, "Okay."

"He reads Dostoevsky day and night."

I knew that he would not ask how I'd come upon this detail. It was a fascinating detail and it was mine, not his, which meant that he would let it pass without comment. But the silence was a brief one.

"Does he have to be Russian to read Dostoevsky?"

"That's not the point. The point is that it all fits together. It's a formulation, it's artful, it's structured."

"He's American, Ilgauskas, same as we are."

"A Russian is always Russian. He even speaks with a slight accent."

"I don't hear an accent."

"You have to listen. It's there," I said.

I didn't know whether it was there or not. The Norway maple didn't have to be Norway. We worked spontaneous variations on the source material of our surroundings.

"You say the man lives in that house. I accept this," I said. "I say he lives there with his son and his son's wife. Her name is Irina."

"And the son. Ilgauskas, so called. His first name?"

"We don't need a first name. He's Ilgauskas. That's all we need," I said.

His hair was mussed, suit jacket dusty and stained, ready to come apart at the shoulder seams. He leaned into the table, square-jawed, sleepy-looking.

"If we isolate the stray thought, the passing thought," he said, "the thought whose origin is unfathomable, then we begin to understand that we are routinely deranged, every-day crazy."

We loved the idea of being everyday crazy. It rang so true, so real.

"In our privatest mind," he said, "there is only chaos and blur. We invented logic to beat back our creatural selves. We assert or deny. We follow M with N."

Our privatest mind, we thought. Did he really say that?

"The only laws that matter are laws of thought."

His fists were clenched on the tabletop, knuckles white.

"The rest is devil worship," he said.

We went walking but did not see the man. The wreaths were mostly gone from the front doors and the occasional bundled figure scraped snow off a car's windshield. Over time we began to understand that these walks were not casual off-campus rambles. We were not looking at trees or boxcars, as we normally did, naming, counting, categorizing. This was different. There was a measure to the man in the hooded coat, old stooped body, face framed in monkish cloth, a history, a faded drama. We wanted to see him one more time.

We agreed on this, Todd and I, and collaborated, in the meantime, on describing his day.

He drinks coffee black, from a small cup, and spoons cereal out of a child's bowl. His head practically rests in the bowl when he bends to eat. He never looks at a newspaper. He goes back to his room after breakfast, where he sits and thinks. His daughter-in-law comes in and makes the bed, Irina, although Todd did not concede the binding nature of the name.

Some days we had to wrap scarves around our faces and speak in muffled voices, only our eyes exposed to the street and the weather.

There are two schoolchildren and one smaller girl, Irina's sister's child, here for reasons not yet determined, and the old man often passes the morning fitfully watching TV cartoons with the child, though not seated beside her. He occupies an armchair well away from the TV set, dozing now and then. Mouth open, we said. Head tilted and mouth hanging open.

We weren't sure why we were doing this. But we tried to be scrupulous, adding new elements every day, making adjustments and refinements, and all the while scanning the streets, trying to induce an appearance through joint force of will.

Soup for lunch, every day it's soup, homemade, and he holds his big spoon over the soup bowl, the old-country bowl, in a manner not unlike the child's, ready to plant a trowel and scoop.

Todd said that Russia was too big for the man. He'd get lost in the vast expanse. Think about Romania, Bulgaria. Better yet, Albania. Is he a Christian, a Muslim? With Albania, he said, we deepen the cultural context. *Context* was his fall-back word.

When he is ready for his walk, Irina tries to help him button his parka, his anorak, but he shakes her off with a few brusque words. She shrugs and replies in kind.

I realized I'd forgotten to tell Todd that Ilgauskas reads Dostoevsky in the original. This was a feasible truth, a usable truth. It made Ilgauskas, in context, a Russian.

He wears trousers with suspenders, until we decided he didn't; it was too close to stereotype. Who shaves the old man? Does he do it himself? We didn't want him to. But who does it and how often?

This was my crystalline link, the old man to Ilgauskas to Dostoevsky to Russia. I thought about it all the time. Todd said it would become my life's work. I would spend my life in a thought bubble, purifying the link.

He doesn't have a private toilet. He shares a toilet with the children but never seems to use it. He is as close to being invisible as a man can get in a household of six. Sitting, thinking, disappearing on his walk.

We shared a vision of the man in his bed, at night, mind roaming back—the village, the hills, the family dead. We walked the same streets every day, obsessively, and we spoke in subdued tones even when we disagreed. It was part of the dialectic, our looks of thoughtful disapproval.

He probably smells bad but the only one who seems to notice is the oldest child, a girl, thirteen. She makes faces now and then, passing behind his chair at the dinner table.

It was the tenth straight sunless day. The number was arbitrary but the mood was beginning to bear in, not the cold or the wind but the missing light, the missing man. Our voices took on an anxious cadence. It occurred to us that he might be dead.

We talked about this all the way back to campus.

Do we make him dead? Do we keep assembling the life posthumously? Or do we end it now, tomorrow, the next day, stop coming to town, stop looking for him? One thing I knew. He does not die Albanian.

The next day, we stood at the end of the street where the designated house was located. We were there for an hour, barely speaking. Were we waiting for him to appear? I don't think we knew. What if he came out of the wrong house? What would this mean? What if someone else came out of the designated house, a young couple carrying ski equipment toward the car in the driveway? Maybe we were there simply to show deferential regard, standing quietly in the presence of the dead.

No one emerged, no one went in, and we left feeling unsure of ourselves.

Minutes later, approaching the railroad tracks, we saw him. We stopped and pointed at each other, holding the pose a moment. It was enormously satisfying, it was thrilling, to see the thing happen, see it become three-dimensional. He made a turn into a street at a right angle to the one we were on. Todd hit me on the arm, turned and started jogging. Then I started jogging. We were going back in the direction we'd just come from. We went around one corner, ran down the street, went around another corner and waited. In time he appeared, walking now in our direction.

This was what Todd wanted, to see him head on. We moved toward him. He seemed to walk a sort of pensive route, meandering with his thoughts. I pulled Todd toward the curb with me so that the man would not have to pass between us. We waited for him to see us. We could almost count off the footsteps to the instant when he would raise his head. It was an interval drawn taut with detail. We were close enough to see the sunken face, heavily stubbled, pinched in around the mouth, jaw sagging. He saw us now and paused, one hand gripping a button at the front of his coat. He looked haunted inside the shabby hood. He looked misplaced, isolated, someone who could easily be the man we were in the process of imagining.

We walked on past and continued for eight or nine paces, then turned and watched.

"That was good," Todd said. "That was totally worthwhile. Now we're ready to take the next step."

"There is no next step. We got our close look," I said. "We know who he is."

"We don't know anything."

"We wanted to see him one more time."

"Lasted only seconds."

"What do you want to do, take a picture?"

"My cell phone needs recharging," he said seriously. "The coat is an anorak, by the way, definitely, up close."

"The coat is a parka."

The man was two and a half blocks from the left turn that would put him on the street where he lived.

"I think we need to take the next step."

"You said that."

"I think we need to talk to him."

I looked at Todd. He wore a fixed smile, grafted on.

"That's crazy."

"It's completely reasonable," he said.

"We do that, we kill the idea, we kill everything we've done. We can't talk to him."

"We'll ask a few questions, that's all. Quiet, low key. Find out a few things."

"It's never been a matter of literal answers."

"I counted eighty-seven boxcars. You counted eighty-seven boxcars. Remember."

"This is different and we both know it."

"I can't believe you're not curious. All we're doing is searching out the parallel life," he said. "It doesn't affect what we've been saying all this time."

"It affects everything. It's a violation. It's crazy."

I looked down the street toward the man in question. He was still moving slowly, a little erratically, hands folded behind his back now, where they belonged.

"If you're sensitive about approaching him, I'll do it," he said.

"No, you won't."

"Why not?"

"Because he's old and frail. Because he won't understand what you want."

"What do I want? A few words of conversation. If he shies away, I'm out of there in an instant."

"Because he doesn't even speak English."

"You don't know that. You don't know anything."

He started to move away and I clutched his arm and turned him toward me.

"Because you'll scare him," I said. "Just the sight of you. Freak of nature."

He looked straight into me. It took time, this look. Then he pulled his arm away and I shoved him into the street. He turned and started walking and I caught up with him and spun him around and struck him in the chest with the heel of my hand. It was a sample blow, an introduction. A car came toward us and veered away, faces in windows. We began to grapple. He was too awkward to be contained, all angles, a mess of elbows and knees, and deceptively strong. I had trouble getting a firm grip and lost a glove. I wanted to hit him in the liver but didn't know where it was. He began flailing in slow motion. I moved in and punched him on the side of the head with my bare hand. It hurt us both and he made a sound and went into a fetal crouch. I snatched his cap and tossed it. I wanted to wrestle him down and pound his head into the asphalt but he was too firmly set, still making the sound, a determined hum, science fiction. He unfolded then, flushed and wild-eyed, and started swinging blind. I stepped back and half circled, waiting for an opening, but he fell before I could hit him, scrambling up at once and starting to run.

The hooded man was about to move out of sight, turning into his street. I watched Todd run, long slack bouncy strides. He would have to go faster if he expected to reach the man before he disappeared into the gray frame house, the designated house.

I saw my lost glove lying in the middle of the street. Then Todd running, bareheaded, trying to skirt areas of frozen snow. The scene empty everywhere around him. I couldn't make sense of it. I felt completely detached. His breath visible, streams of trailing vapor. I wondered what it was that had caused this thing to happen. He only wanted to talk to the man.

HAMMER
AND SICKLE

We walked across the highway bridge, thirty-nine of us in jumpsuits and tennis sneakers, with guards front and back and at the flanks, six in all. Beneath us the cars were blasting by, nonstop, their speed magnified by our near vantage and by the sound they made passing under the low bridge. There's no word for it, that sound, pure urgency, sustained, incessant, northbound, southbound, and each time we walked across the overpass I wondered again who those people were, the drivers and passengers, so many cars, the pressing nature of their passage, the lives inside.

I had time to notice such things, time to reflect. It's a killing business, reflection, even in the lowest levels of security, where there are distractions, openings into the former world. The inmate soccer game at the abandoned high school field across the highway was a breezy departure from the daily binding and squeezing of meal lines, head counts, regulations, reflections. The players rode a bus, the spectators walked, the cars zoomed beneath the bridge.

I walked alongside a man named Sylvan Telfair, tall, bald, steeped in pathos, an international banker who'd dealt in rarefied instruments of offshore finance.

"You follow soccer?"

"I don't follow anything," he said.

"But it's worth watching under the circumstances, right? Which is exactly how I feel."

"I follow nothing," he said.

"My name's Jerold."

"Very good," he said.

The camp was not enclosed by stone walls or coiled razor wire. The only perimeter fencing was a scenic artifact now, a set of old wooden posts that supported sagging rails. There were four dormitories with bunk-bed cubicles, toilets and showers. There were several structures to accommodate inmate orientation, meals, medical care, TV viewing, gym work, visits from family and others. There were conjugal hours for those so yoked.

"You can call me Jerry," I said.

I knew that Sylvan Telfair had been denied a special detention suite with audiovisual systems, private bath, smoking privileges and a toaster oven. There were only four of these in the camp and the man seemed, in bearing alone, in his emotional distance and discreet pain, to be entitled to special consideration. Stuck in the dorms, I thought. This must have seemed a life sentence wedged into the nine years he'd brought with him from Switzerland or Liechtenstein or the Cayman Islands.

I wanted to know something about the man's methodology, the arc of his crimes, but I was reluctant to ask and he was certain not to answer. I'd been here only two months and was still trying to figure out who I wanted to be in this setting, how I ought to stand, sit, walk, talk. Sylvan Telfair knew who he was. He was a long-striding man in a well-pressed jumpsuit and spotless white sneakers, laces knotted oddly behind the ankles, a man formally absent from his slightest word or gesture.

The traffic noise was a ripple at the treetops by the time we reached the edge of the camp complex.

When I was in my early teens I came across the word *phantasm*. A great word, I thought, and I wanted to be phantasmal, someone who slips in and out of physical reality. Now here I am, a floating fever dream, but where's the rest of it, the dense surround, the thing with weight and heft? There's a man here who aspires to be a biblical scholar. His head is bent severely to one side, nearly resting on his left shoulder, the result of an unnamed affliction. I admire the man, I'd like to talk to him, tilting my head slightly, feeling secure in the depths of his scholarship, the languages, cultures, documents, rituals. And the head itself, is there anything here more real than this?

There's another man who runs everywhere, the Dumb Runner he's called, but he's doing something obsessive and true, outside the margins of our daily protocols. He has a heartbeat, a racing pulse. And then the gamblers, men betting surreptitiously on football, engaged all week in the crosstalk of point spreads, bunk to bunk, meal to meal, Eagles minus four, Rams getting eight and a half. Is this virtual money they're betting? Stand near them when they talk and it's real, touchable, and so are they, gesturing operatically, numbers flashing neon in the air.

We watched TV in one of the common rooms. There was a large flat screen, wall-mounted, certain channels blocked, programs selected by one of the veteran inmates, a different man each month. On this day only five places were occupied in the eighty or so folding chairs in the arched rows. I was here to see a particular program, an afternoon news broadcast, fifteen minutes, on a children's channel. One segment was a stock market report. Two girls, earnestly amateurish, reported on the day's market activity.

I was the only one watching the show. The other inmates sat half dazed, heads down. It was a matter of time of day, time of year, dusk nearly upon us, the depressive specter of last light stirring at the oblong windows high on one wall. The men sat distanced from each other, here to be alone. This was the call to self-examination, the second-guessing of a lost life, no less compelling than the believer's call to prayer.

I watched and listened. The girls were my daughters, Laurie and Kate, ten and twelve. Their mother had told me, curtly, over the phone, that the kids had been selected to appear on such a program. No details available, she said, at the present time, as if she were reporting, herself, from a desk in a studio humming with off-camera tensions.

I sat in the second row, alone, and there they were, sharing a table, speaking about fourth-quarter estimates, first one girl, then the other, a couple of sentences at a time, credit quality, credit demand, the tech sector, the budget deficit. The picture had the quality of online video, user-generated. I tried to detach myself, to see the girls as distant references to my daughters, in jittery black and white. I studied them. I observed. They read their lines from pages held in their hands, each looking up from the page as she yielded to the other reader.

Did it seem crazy, a market report for kids? There was nothing sweet or charming about the commentary. The girls were not playing at being adult. They were dutiful, blending occasional definitions and explanations into the news, and then Laurie's eyes showed fleeting panic in her remarks about the Nasdaq Composite—a mangled word, a missing sentence. I took the report to be a tentative segment of a barely noticed show on an obscure cable channel. It wasn't any crazier, probably, than most TV, and anyway who was watching?

My bunkmate wore socks to bed. He tucked his pajama legs into the socks and lay on his bunk, knees up and hands folded behind his head.

"I miss my walls," he said.

He had the lower bunk. This was a matter of some significance in the camp, top or bottom, who gets what, like every prison movie we'd ever seen. Norman was senior to me in age, experience, ego and time served and I had no reason to complain.

I thought of telling him that we all miss our walls, we miss our floors and ceilings. But I sat and waited for him to continue.

"I used to sit and look. One wall, then another. After a while I'd get up and walk around the apartment, slowly, looking, wall to wall. Sit and look, stand and look."

He seemed to be under a spell, reciting a bedtime story he'd heard as a child.

"You collected art, is that it?"

"That's it, past tense, collected. Major museum quality."

"You've never mentioned this," I said.

"I've been here how long? They're somebody else's walls now. The art is scattered."

"You had advisers, experts on the art market."

"People used to come and look at my walls. Europe, Los Angeles, a Japanese man from some foundation in Japan."

He sat quietly for a time, remembering. I found myself remembering with him. The Japanese man took on facial features, a certain size and shape, portly, it seemed, pale suit, dark tie.

"Collectors, curators, students. They came and looked," he said.

"Who advised you?"

"I had a woman on Fifty-seventh Street. There was a guy in London, Colin, knew everything about the Postimpressionists. A dear sweet man."

"You don't really mean that."

"It's something people say. One of those expressions that sound like someone else is talking. A dear sweet man."

"A loving wife and mother."

"I was happy to have them look. All of them," he said. "I used to look with them. We'd go picture to picture, room to room. I had a house in the Hudson Valley, more paintings, some sculpture. I went there in the autumn for the fall colors. But I barely looked out the windows."

"You had the walls."

"I couldn't take my eyes off the walls."

"And then you had to sell."

"All of it, every last piece. Pay fines, pay debts, pay legal fees, provide for family. Gave an etching to my daughter. A snowy night in Norway."

Norman missed his walls but he was not unhappy here. He

was content, he said, unstuck, unbound, remote. He was free of the swollen needs and demands of others but mostly disentangled from his personal drives, his grabbiness, the lifelong mandate to accrue, expand, construct himself, to buy a hotel chain, make a name. He was at peace here, he said.

I lay on the top bunk, eyes closed, listening. Throughout the building men in their cubicles, one talking, one listening, both silent, one sleeping, tax delinquents, alimony delinquents, insider traders, perjurers, hedge-fund felons, mail fraud, mortgage fraud, securities fraud, accounting fraud, obstruction of justice.

Word began to spread. By the third day most of the chairs in the common room were occupied and I had to settle for a place near the end of the fifth row. On screen the girls were reporting on a situation rapidly developing in the Arab Emirates.

"The word is Dubai."

"This is the word crossing continents and oceans at the shocking speed of light."

"Markets are sinking quickly."

"Paris, Frankfurt, London."

"Dubai has the worst debt per capita in the world," Kate said. "And now its building boom has crumbled and it can't pay the banks what it owes them."

"It owes them fifty-eight billion dollars," Laurie said.

"Give or take a few billion."

"The DAX index in Germany."

"Down more than three percent."

"The Royal Bank of Scotland."

"Down more than four percent."

153

"The word is Dubai."

"This debt-ridden city-state is asking banks to grant six months' freedom from debt repayments."

"Dubai," Laurie said.

"The cost of insuring Dubai's debt against default has increased one, two, three, four times."

"Do we know what that means?"

"It means the Dow Jones Industrial Average is down, down, down."

"Deutsche Bank."

"Down."

"London—the FTSE One Hundred Index."

"Down."

"Amsterdam—ING Group."

"Down."

"The Hang Seng in Hong Kong."

"Crude oil. Islamic bonds."

"Down, down, down."

"The word is Dubai."

"Say it."

"Dubai," Kate said.

The old life rewrites itself every minute. In four years I'll still be here, puddling horribly in this dim waste. The free future is hard to imagine. I have trouble enough tracing the shape of the knowable past. This is no steadfast element, no faith or truth except for the girls, being born, getting bigger, living.

Where was I when this was happening? I was acquiring meaningless degrees, teaching a freshman course in the dynamics of reality TV. I changed the spelling of my first name to Jerold. I used my index and middle fingers to place quote marks around certain ironic comments I made and sometimes used index fingers only, setting off a quotation within another quotation. It was that kind of life, self-mocking, and neither the marriage nor the business I briefly ran seems to have happened in any fixed consideration. I'm thirty-nine years old, a generation removed from some of the inmates here, and I don't remember knowing why I did what I did to put myself in this place. There was a time in early English law when a felony was punishable by removal of one of the felon's body parts. Would this be an incentive to modern memory?

I imagine myself being here forever, it's already forever, eating another meal with the political consultant who licks his thumb to pick bread crumbs off the plate and stare at them, or standing in line behind the investment banker who talks to himself aloud in beginner's Mandarin. I think about money. What did I know about it, how much did I need it, what would I do when I got it? Then I think about Sylvan Telfair, aloof in his craving, the billion-euro profit being separable from the things it bought, money the coded impulse, ideational, a kind of discreet erection known only to the man whose pants are on fire.

"The fear continues to grow."

"Fear of numbers, fear of spreading losses."

"The fear is Dubai. The talk is Dubai. Dubai has the debt. Is it fifty-eight billion dollars or eighty billion dollars?"

"Bankers are pacing marble floors."

"Or is it one hundred and twenty billion dollars?"

"Sheiks are gazing into hazy skies."

"Even the numbers are panicking."

"Think of the prominent investors. Hollywood stars. Famous footballers."

"Think of islands shaped like palm trees. People skiing in a shopping mall."

"The world's only seven-star hotel."

"The world's richest horse race."

"The world's tallest building."

"All this in Dubai."

"Taller than the Empire State Building and the Chrysler Building combined."

"Combined."

"Swim in the pool on the seventy-sixth floor. Pray in the mosque on the one hundred and fifty-eighth floor."

"But where is the oil?"

"Dubai has no oil. Dubai has debt. Dubai has a huge number of foreign workers with nowhere to work."

"Enormous office buildings stand empty. Apartment buildings unfinished in blowing sand. Think of the blowing sand. Dust storms concealing the landscape. Empty storefronts in every direction."

"But where is the oil?"

"The oil is in Abu Dhabi. Say the name."

"Abu Dhabi."

"Now let's say it together."

"Abu Dhabi," they said.

It was Feliks Zuber, the oldest inmate at the camp, who'd chosen the children's program for viewing. Feliks was here every day now, front row center, carrying with him a sentence of seven hundred and twenty years. He liked to turn and nod at those nearby, making occasional applause gestures without bringing his trembling hands into contact, a small crumpled man, looking nearly old enough to be on the verge of outliving his sentence, tinted glasses, purple jumpsuit, hair dyed death black.

The length of his sentence impressed the rest of us. It was a term handed down for his master manipulation of an investment scheme involving four countries and leading to the collapse of two governments and three corporations, with much of the money channeled in the direction of arms shipments to rebels in a breakaway enclave of the Caucasus.

The breadth of his crimes warranted a far more stringent environment than this one but he'd been sent here because he was riddled with disease, his future marked in weeks and days. Men were sometimes sent here to die, in easeful circumstances. We knew it from their faces, mainly, the attenuated range of vision, the sensory withdrawal, and from the stillness they brought with them, a cloistered manner, as if bound by vows. Feliks was not still. He smiled, waved, bounced and shook. He sat on the edge of his chair when the girls delivered news of falling markets and stunned economies. He was a man watching an ancient truism unfold on wide-screen TV. He would take the world with him when he died.

The soccer field was part of a haunted campus. A grade school and high school had been closed because the county did not have the resources to maintain them. The antiquated buildings were partly demolished now, a few wrecking machines still there, asquat in mud.

The inmates were glad to keep the field in playable condition, chalking the lines and arcs, planting corner flags, sinking the goals firmly in the ground. The games were an earnest pastime for the players, men mostly middle-aged, a few older, two or three younger, all in makeshift uniforms, running, standing, walking, crouching, often simply bending from the waist, breathless, hands on knees, looking into the scuffed turf where their lives were mired.

There were fewer spectators as the days grew colder, then fewer players. I kept showing up, blowing on my hands, beating my arms across my chest. The teams were coached by inmates, the games refereed by inmates, and those of us watching from the three rows of old broken bleacher seats were inmates. The guards stood around, here and there, watching and not.

The games became stranger. Rules were invented, broken and abridged, a fight started now and then, the game going on around it. I kept waiting for a player to be stricken, a heart attack, a convulsive collapse. The spectators rarely cheered or moaned. It began to feel like nowhere, men moving in the dreamy distance, linesmen sharing a cigarette. We walked across the bridge, watched the game, walked back across the bridge.

I thought about soccer in history, the inspiration for wars, truces, rampaging mobs. The game was a global passion, spherical ball, grass or turf, entire nations in spasms of elation or lament. But what kind of sport is it that disallows the use of players' hands, except for the goalkeeper? Hands are essential human tools, the things that grasp and hold, that make, take, carry, create. If soccer were an American invention, wouldn't some European intellectual maintain that our historically puritanical nature has compelled us to invent a game structured on anti-masturbatory principles?

This is one of the things I think about that I never had to think about before.

The notable thing about Norman Bloch, my bunkmate, was not the art that used to hang on his walls. What impressed me was the crime he'd committed. This was itself a kind of art, conceptual in nature, radical in scale, a deed so casual and yet so transgressive that Norman, here a year, would be spending six more years in the camp, the bunk, the clinic, the meal lines, in the squalling noise of the hand dryers in the toilets.

Norman did not pay taxes. He did not file quarterly reports or annual returns and he did not request extensions. He did not backdate documents, establish trusts or foundations, open secret accounts or utilize the ready mechanisms of offshore jurisdictions. He was not a political or religious protester. He was not a nihilist, rejecting all values and institutions. He was completely transparent. He just didn't pay. It was a kind of lethargy, he said, the way people avoid doing the dishes or making the bed.

I brightened at that. Doing the dishes, making the bed. He said he didn't know exactly how long it was since he'd last paid taxes. When I asked about his financial advisers, his business associates, he shrugged, or so I imagined. I was in the top bunk, he was in the bottom, two men in pajamas, passing the time.

"Those girls. Pretty amazing," he said. "And the news, especially the bad news."

"You like the bad news."

"We all like the bad news. Even the girls like the bad news."

I thought of telling him that they were my daughters. No one here knew this and it was better that way. I didn't want the men in the dorm looking at me, talking to me, spreading the word throughout the camp. I was learning how to disappear. It suited me, it was my natural state, day by day, to be phantasmal again.

Best not to speak of the girls.

Then I spoke of them, quietly, in six or seven words. There was a long pause. He had a round face, Norman, with a squat nose, his bushy hair going gray.

"You never said this, Jerry."

"Just between us."

"You never say anything."

"Just to you. No one else. It's true," I said. "Kate and Laurie. I sit and watch them and it's hard to understand how any of this happened. What are they doing there, what am I doing here? Their mother writes the reports. She didn't tell me this but I know it's her. She's masterminding the whole thing."

"What's she like, their mother?"

"We're legally separated."

"What's she like?" he said.

"Fairly smart, like in a cutting-edge way. Sneaky sort of pretty. You have to pay attention to see it."

"You still love her? I don't think I ever loved my wife. Not in the original meaning of the word."

I didn't ask what he meant by that.

"Did your wife love you?"

"She loved my walls," he said.

"I love my kids."

"You love their mother too. I can sense it," he said.

"From where, the lower bunk? You can't even see my face."

"I've seen your face. What's to see?"

"We fell apart. We didn't drift apart, we fell apart."

"Don't tell me I'm not right. I sense things. I read into things," he said.

I looked into the ceiling. It had rained for several hours and I thought I could hear traffic noise on the wet highway, cars racing beneath the overpass, drivers leaning into the night, trying to read the road at every flex and bend.

"I'll tell you what it's like. It's like they're playing a game," he said. "All those names they're saying. The Hang Seng in Hong Kong. That's funny to a kid. And when kids say it, it's funny to us. And I'll make you a bet. Plenty of kids are watching that report and not because it's on a kids' channel. They're watching because it's funny. What the hell's the Hang Seng in Hong Kong? I don't know. Do you know?"

"Their mother knows."

"I'll bet she does. She also knows it's a game, all of it. And all of it's funny. You're lucky," he said. "Terrific kids."

Happy here, that was Norman. We're not in prison, he liked to say. We're at camp.

Over time the situation in the Gulf began to ease. Abu Dhabi provided a ten-billion-dollar bailout and relative calm soon moved into the Gulf and across the digital networks to markets everywhere. This brought on a letdown in the common room. Even as the girls showed improvement in their delivery and signs of serious preparation, the men stopped coming in large numbers and soon there was only a scatter of us, here and there, sleepy and reflective.

* * *

We had TV but what had we lost, all of us, when we entered the camp? We'd lost our appendages, our extensions, the data systems that kept us fed and cleansed. Where was the world, our world? The laptops were gone, the smartphones and light sensors and megapixels. Our hands and eyes needed more than we could give them now. The touch screens, the mobile platforms, the gentle bell reminders of an appointment or a flight time or a woman in a room somewhere. And the sense, the tacit awareness, now lost, that something newer, smarter, faster, ever faster, was just a bird's breath away. Also lost was the techno-anxiety that these devices routinely carried with them. But we needed this no less than the devices themselves, that inherent stress, those cautions and frustrations. Weren't these essential to our mind-set? The prospect of failed signals and crashed systems, the memory that needs recharging, the identity stolen in a series of clicks. Information, this was everything, coming in, going out. We were always on, wanted to be on, needed to be on, but this was history now, the shadow of another life.

Okay, we were grown-ups, not bug-eyed kids in tribal bondage, and this was not an Internet rescue camp. We lived in real space, unaddicted, free of deadly dependence. But we were bereft. We were pulpy and slumped. It was a thing we rarely talked about, a thing that was hard to shake. There were the small idle moments when we knew exactly what we were missing. We sat on the toilet, flushed and done, staring into empty hands.

I wanted to find myself in front of the TV set for the market report, weekdays, four in the afternoon, but could not always manage. I was part of a work detail that was bused on designated days to the adjacent Air Force base, where we sanded and painted, did general maintenance, hauled garbage and sometimes just stood and watched as a fighter jet roared down the runway and lifted into the low sun. It was a beautiful thing to see, aircraft climbing, wheels up, wings pivoting back, the light, the streaked sky, three or four of us, not a word spoken. Was this the time, more than a thousand other moments, when the measure of our ruin was brought to starkest awareness?

"All of Europe is looking south. What do they see?"

"They see Greece."

"They see fiscal instability, enormous debt burden, possible default."

"*Crisis* is a Greek word."

"Is Greece hiding its public debt?"

"Is the crisis spreading at lightning speed to the rest of the southern tier, to the euro zone in general, to emerging markets everywhere?"

"Does Greece need a bailout?"

"Will Greece abandon the euro?"

"Did Greece hide the nature of its debt?"

"What is Wall Street's role in this critical matter?"

"What is a credit default swap? What is a sovereign default? What is a special-purpose entity?"

"We don't know. Do you know? Do you care?"

"What is Wall Street? Who is Wall Street?"

Tense laughter from pockets in the audience.

"Greece, Portugal, Spain, Italy."

"Stocks plunge worldwide."

"The Dow, the Nasdaq, the euro, the pound."

"But where are the walkouts, the work stoppages, the job actions?"

"Look at Greece. Look in the streets."

"Riots, strikes, protests, pickets."

"All of Europe is looking at Greece."

"*Chaos* is a Greek word."

"Canceled flights, burning flags, stones flying this way, tear gas sailing that way."

"Workers are angry. Workers are marching."

"Blame the worker. Bury the worker."

"Freeze their pay. Increase their tax."

"Steal from the worker. Screw the worker."

"Any day now, wait and see."

"New flags, new banners."

"Hammer and sickle."

"Hammer and sickle."

Their mother had the girls delivering lines in a balanced flow, a cadence. They weren't just reading, they were acting, showing facial expression, having serious fun. Screw the worker, Kate had said. At least their mother had assigned the vulgar line to the older girl.

Was the daily market report becoming a performance piece?

All day long the story passed through the camp, building to building, man to man. It concerned a convict on death row in Texas or Missouri or Oklahoma and the last words he'd spoken before an individual authorized by the state injected the lethal substance or activated the electric current.

The words were, *Kick the tires and light the fire—I'm going home.*

Some of us felt a chill, hearing the story. Were we shamed by it? Did we think of that man on the honed edge of his last breath as more authentic than we were, a true outlaw, worthy of the state's most cruelly scrupulous attention? His end was officially sanctioned, an act welcomed by some, protested by some. If he'd spent half a lifetime in prison cells, in solitary confinement and finally on death row for one or two or multiple homicides, where were we and what had we done to be placed here? Did we even remember our crimes? Could we call them crimes? They were loopholes, evasions, wheedling half-ass felonies.

Some of us, less self-demeaning, simply nodded at the story, conveying simple credit to the man for the honor he'd brought to the moment, the back-country poetry of those words. By the third time I heard the story, or overheard it, the prison was located decisively in Texas. Forget the other places—the man, the story and the prison all belonged in Texas. We were somewhere else, watching a children's program on TV.

"What's this business about hammer and sickle?"

"Means nothing. Words," I said. "Like Abu Dhabi."

"The Hang Seng in Hong Kong."

"Exactly."

"The girls like saying it. Hammer and sickle."

"Hammer and sickle."

"Abu Dhabi."

"Abu Dhabi."

"Hang Seng."

"Hong Kong," I said.

We went on like that for a while. Norman was still murmuring the names when I shut my eyes and began the long turn toward sleep.

"But I think she means it. I think she's serious. Hammer and sickle," he said. "She's a serious woman with a point to make."

I stood watching from a distance. They passed through the metal detector, one by one, and moved toward the visitors' center, the wives and children, the loyal friends, the business partners, the lawyers who would sit and listen in a confidential setting as inmates stared at them through tight eyes and complained about the food, the job assignments, the scarcity of sentence reductions.

Everything seemed flat. The visitors on the footpath moved slowly and monochromatically. The sky was barely there, drained of light and weather. Families were bundled and wan but I didn't feel the cold. I was standing outside the dormitory but could have been anywhere. I imagined a woman walking among the others, slim and dark-haired, unaccompanied. I don't know where she came from, a photograph I'd once seen, or a movie, possibly French, set in Southeast Asia, sex beneath a ceiling fan. Here, she was wearing a long white tunic and loose trousers. She belonged to another setting, this was clear, but there was no need for me to wonder what she was doing here. She'd come up out of the drowsy mind or down from the flat sky.

There was a name for the outfit she was wearing and I nearly knew it, nearly had it, then it slipped away. But the woman was there, still, in pale sandals, the tunic slit on the sides, with a faint floral design front and back.

The ceiling fan turned slowly in the heavy heat, a thought I didn't want or need, but there it was, more thought than image, going back years.

Who was the man she was here to see? I was expecting no visitors, didn't want them, not even my daughters, not right for them to see me here. They were two thousand miles away in any case, and otherwise engaged. Could I place the woman in my immediate presence, face to face across a table in the large open space that would soon be filled with inmates, wives and kids, a guard at an elevated desk, keeping watch?

One thing I knew. The name of her outfit was two words, brief words, and it would make me feel the day was worthwhile, the full week, if I could remember those words. What else was there to do? What else could I think about that might yield a decent measure of completion?

Vietnamese—the words, the tunic, the trousers, the woman.

Then I thought of Sylvan Telfair. He was the inmate she was here to see, a man of worldwide address. They'd met in Paris or Bangkok. They'd stood on a terrace in the evening, sipping wine and speaking French. He was refined and assured and at the same time somewhat reticent, a man to whom she might be attracted, even if she was my idea, my secret silken vision.

I stood watching, thinking.

By the time the words came to me, much later in the day, *ao dai*, I'd lost all interest in the matter.

* * *

We were grouped, clustered, massed, paired, men everywhere, living in swarms, filling every space, arrayed across the limits of vision. I liked to think of us as men in Maoist self-correction, perfecting our social being through repetition. We worked, ate and slept in mechanized routine, weekly, daily, hourly, advancing from practice to knowledge. But these were the musings of idle time. Maybe we were just tons of assimilated meat, our collected flesh built into cubicles, containered in dormitories and dining halls, zippered into jumpsuits in five colors, classified, catalogued, this color for that level of offense. The colors struck me as a kind of comic pathos, always there, brightly clashing, jutting, crisscrossing. I tried not to think of us as circus clowns who'd forgotten their face paint.

"You consider her your enemy," Norman said. "You and her, blood enemies."

"I don't think that's true."

"It's only natural. You think she's using the girls against you. This is what you believe, down deep, whether you admit it or not."

"I don't think that's the case."

"That has to be the case. She's attacking you for the mistakes you made in business. What was your business? How did it get you here? I don't think you ever said."

"It's not interesting."

"We're not here to be interesting."

"I ran a company for a man who acquired companies. Information got passed back and forth. Money changed hands. Lawyers, traders, consultants, senior partners."

"Who was the man?"

"He was my father," I said.

"What's his name?"

"He died quietly before the fact."

"What fact?"

"The fact of my conviction."

"What's his name?"

"Walter Bradway."

"Do I know that name?"

"You know his brother's name. Howard Bradway."

"One of the hedge-fund musketeers," he said.

Norman was searching his memory for visual confirmation. I pictured what he was picturing. He was picturing my uncle Howie, a large ruddy man, barechested, in aviator glasses, with a miniature poodle huddled in the crook of his arm. A fairly famous image.

"A family tradition. Is that it?" he said. "Different companies, different cities, different time frames."

"They believed in right and wrong. The right and wrong of the markets, the portfolios, the insider information."

"Then it was your turn to join the business. Did you know what you were doing?"

"I was defining myself. That's what my father said. He said people who have to define themselves belong in the dictionary."

"Because you strike me as somebody who doesn't always know what he's doing."

"I pretty much knew. I definitely knew."

I could hear Norman unraveling the improvised cellophane wrap on his little jar of fig spread and then using his finger to rub the stuff across a saltine cracker. On visitors' days his lawyer smuggled a jar of Dalmatian fig spread into the camp, minus the metal cap. Norman said he liked the name, Dalmatia, Dalmatian, the Balkan history, the Adriatic, the large spotted dog. He liked the idea of having food of that particular name and place, all natural ingredients, and eating it on a standard cafeteria cracker, undercover, a couple of times a week.

He said that his lawyer was a woman and that she concealed the fig spread somewhere on her body. This was a throwaway line, delivered in a monotone and not intended to be believed.

"What's your philosophy of money?"

"I don't have one," I said.

"There was the year I made a shitpile of money. One year in particular. We could be talking, total, easy nine figures. I could feel it adding years to my life. Money makes you live longer. It seeps into the bloodstream, into the veins and capillaries. I talked to my primary-care physician about this. He said he had an inkling I could be right."

"What about the art on your walls? Make you live longer?"

"I don't know about the art. Good question, the art."

"People say great art is immortal. I say there's something mortal in it. It carries a glimpse of death."

"All those gorgeous paintings, the shapes and colors. All those dead painters. I don't know," he said.

He lifted his hand toward my bunk, up and around, with a splotch of fig preserves on half a cracker. I declined, but thanks. I heard him chewing the cracker and sinking into the sheets. Then I lay waiting for the final remarks of the day.

"She's talking directly to you. You realize this, using the girls."

"I don't think so, not even remotely."

"In other words this never occurred to you."

"Everything occurs to me. Some things I reject."

"What's her name?"

"Sara Massey."

"Good and direct. I see her as a strong woman with roots going back a long way. Principles, convictions. Getting revenge for your illegal activities, for the fact you got caught, maybe for joining your father's business in the first place."

"How smart I am not to know this. What grief it spares me."

"This sneaky-pretty woman in your words. She's reminding you what you did. She's talking to you. Abu Dhabi, Abu Dhabi. Hang Seng, Hong Kong."

All around us, entombed in cubicles, suspended in time, reliably muted now, men with dental issues, medical issues, marital issues, dietary demands, psychic frailties, sleep-breathing men, the nightly drone of oil-tax schemes, tax-shelter schemes, corporate espionage, corporate bribery, false testimony, medicare fraud, inheritance fraud, real estate fraud, wire fraud, fraud and conspiracy.

They started arriving early, men crowding the common room, some carrying extra folding chairs, snapping them open. There were others standing in the side aisles, a spillover of inmates, guards, kitchen staff, camp officials. I'd managed to squeeze into the fourth row, slightly off-center. The sense of event, news in high clamor, all the convergences of emotional global forces bringing us here in a wave of complex expectation.

A cluster of rain-swept blossoms was fixed to one of the high windows. Spring, more or less, late this year.

There were four common rooms, one for each dorm, and I was certain that all were packed, inmates and others collected in some odd harmonic, listening to children talk about economic collapse.

Here, as time approached, Feliks Zuber rose briefly from his seat up front, raising a weary hand to quiet the settling crowd.

I noticed at once that the girls wore matching jackets. This was new. The picture was sharper and steadier, in color. Then I realized they were seated at a long desk, a news desk, not an ordinary table. Finally the scripts—there were no scripts. They were using a teleprompter, delivering lines at fairly high speed with occasional tactical pauses, well placed.

"Greece is selling bonds, raising euros."

"Markets are calming."

"Greece is moving toward a new austerity."

"Immediate pressure is relieved."

"Greece and Germany are talking."

"Votes of confidence. Calls for patience."

"Greece is ready to restore trust."

"Aid package of forty billion dollars."

"How do they say thank you in Greek?"

"*Efharisto.*"

"Say it again, slowly."

"F. Harry Stowe."

"F. Harry Stowe."

They exchanged a fist-bump, deadpan, without looking at each other.

"The worst may be over."

"Or the worst is yet to come."

"Do we know if the Greek bailout will do what it is designed to do?"

"Or will it do just the opposite?"

"What exactly is the opposite?"

"Think about markets elsewhere."

"Is anyone looking at Portugal?"

"Everyone's looking at Portugal."

"High debt, low growth."

"Borrow, borrow, borrow."

"Euro, euro, euro."

"Ireland has a problem. Iceland has a problem."

"Have we thought about the British pound?"

"The life and death of the British pound."

"The pound is not the euro."

"Britain is not Greece."

"But is the pound showing signs of cracking? Will the euro follow? Is the dollar far behind?"

"There is talk about China."

"Is there trouble in China?"

"Is there a bubble in China?"

"What is the Chinese currency called?"

"Latvia has the lat."

"Tonga has the ponga."

"China has the rebimbi."

"The rebimbo."

"China has the rebobo."

"The rebubu."

"What happens next?"

"It already happened."

"Does anyone remember?"

"Market plunges one thousand points in an eighth of a second."

"A tenth of a second."

"Faster and faster, lower and lower."

"A twentieth of a second."

"Screens glow and vibrate, phones jump off walls."

"A hundredth of a second. A thousandth of a second."

"Not real, unreal, surreal."

"Who is doing this? Where is it coming from? Where is it going?"

"It happened in Chicago."

"It happened in Kansas."

"It's a movie, it's a song."

I could feel the mood in the room, a pressing intensity, a need for something more, something stronger. I remained detached, watching the girls, wondering about their mother, what she had in mind, where she was leading us.

Laurie said softly, in a lilting voice: "Who do we trust? Where do we turn? How do we ever get to sleep?"

Kate said briskly, "Can computer technology keep up with computerized trading? Will long-term doubts yield to short-term doubts?"

"What is a fat-finger trade? What is a naked short sale?"

"How many trillions of dollars pledged to bleeding euro economies?"

"How many zeros is a trillion?"

"How many meetings deep in the night?"

"Why does the crisis keep getting worse?"

"Brazil, Korea, Japan, Wherever."

"What are they doing and where are they doing it?"

"They're on strike again in Greece."

"They're marching in the streets."

"They're burning banks in Greece."

"They're hanging banners from sacred temples."

"Peoples of Europe, rise up."

"Peoples of the world, unite."

"The tide is rising, the tide is turning."

"Which way? How fast?"

There was a long pause. We watched and waited. Then the news report reached its defining moment, do-or-die, the point of no return.

The girls recited together:

"Stalin Khrushchev Castro Mao."

"Lenin Brezhnev Engels—Pow!"

These names, that exclamation, delivered in rapid sing-song, roused the inmates to spontaneous noise. What kind of noise was it? What did it mean? I sat stone-faced, in the middle of it, trying to understand. The girls repeated the lines once, then again. The men yelled and clamored, these flabby white-collar felons, seeming to reject everything they'd believed all their lives.

"Brezhnev Khrushchev Mao and Ho."

"Lenin Stalin Castro Zhou."

The names kept coming. It resembled a school chant, the cry of leaping cheerleaders, and the men's response grew in volume and feeling. It was tremendous, totally, and it scared me. What did these names mean to the inmates? We were a long way from the funny place-names of earlier reports. These names were immense imprints on history. Did the inmates want to replace one doctrine, one system of government with another? We were the end products of the system, the logical outcome, slabs of burnt-out capital. We were also men with families and homes, whatever our present situation. We had beliefs, commitments. It went beyond systems, I thought. They were asserting that nothing mattered, that distinctions were dead. Let the markets crash and die. Let the banks, the brokerage firms, the groups, the funds, the trusts, the institutes all turn to dust.

"*Mao Zhou — Fidel Ho.*"

The aisles, meanwhile, were still and hushed — guards, doctors, camp administrators. I wanted it to be over. I wanted the girls to go home, do their homework, withdraw into their cell phones.

"*Marx Lenin Che — Hey!*"

Their mother was crazy, perverting the novelty of a children's stock market report. The inmates were confused, stirring themselves into mindless anarchy. Only Feliks Zuber made sense, pumping his fist, feebly, a man who was here for attempting to finance a revolution, able to hear trumpets and drums in that chorus of names. It took a while before the energy in the room began to recede, the girls' voices becoming calmer now.

"We're all waiting for an answer."

"Accordingly, analysts say."

"Eventually, investors maintain."

"Elsewhere, economists claim."

"Somewhere, officials insist."

"This could be bad," Kate said.

"How bad?"

"Very bad."

"How bad?"

"End-of-the-world bad."

They stared into the camera, finishing in a whisper.

"F. Harry Stowe."

"F. Harry Stowe."

The report was over but the girls remained onscreen. They sat looking, we sat looking. The moment became uneasy. Laurie glanced to the side and then slid off her chair and moved out of camera range. Kate stayed put. I watched a familiar look slide into her eyes and across her mouth and jaw. This was the look of noncompliance. Why should she submit to an embarrassing exit caused by some dumb technical blunder? She would stare us all down. Then she would tell us exactly how she felt about the matter, about the show itself and the news itself. This is what made me want to get up and leave, to slip unnoticed out of the row and along the wall and into the dusty light of late afternoon. But I stayed and looked and so did she. We were looking at each other. She leaned forward now, placing her elbows on the desk, hands folded at chin level like a fifth-grade teacher impatient with my snickering and fidgeting or just my stupidity. The tension in the room had mass and weight. This is what I feared, that she would speak about the news, all news all the time, and about how her father always said that the news exists so it can disappear, this is the point of news, whatever story, wherever it is happening. *We depend on the news to disappear,* my father says. *Then my father became the news. Then he disappeared.*

But she only sat and looked and soon the inmates began to get restless. I realized that my hand was covering the lower part of my face, in needless parental disguise. People, a few at a time, then more, then groups, all leaving now, some crouching down as they moved between the rows. Maybe they were being careful not to block the view of others but I thought that most were slinking out, in guilt and shame. Either way, the view stayed the same, Kate on camera, sitting there looking at me. I felt hollowed out but I couldn't leave while she was still there. I waited for the screen to go blank and finally, long minutes later, that's what happened, in streaks and tremors.

The room had emptied out by the time a cartoon appeared, a fat boy rolling down a bumpy hill. Feliks Zuber was still in his seat up front, he and I in lone attendance now, and I waited for him to turn and wave at me, or simply sit there, dead.

I opened my eyes sometime before first light and the dream was still there, hovering, nearly touchable. We can't do justice to our dreams, reworking them in memory. They seem borrowed, part of another life, ours only maybe and only in the farthest margins. A woman is standing beneath a ceiling fan in a tall shadowy room in Ho Chi Minh City, the name of the city indelibly webbed within the dream, and the woman, momentarily obscured, is stepping out of her sandals and beginning to look familiar, and now I realize why this is so, because she is my wife, very weirdly, Sara Massey, slowly shedding her clothing, a tunic and loose trousers, an *ao dai*.

Was this meant to be erotic, or ironic, or just another random package of cranial debris? Thinking about it made me edgy and after a moment I lowered myself from the end of the top bunk, quietly. Norman lay still, wearing a black sleep mask. I dressed and left the cubicle and went across the floor and out into the predawn mist. The guardpost at the camp entrance was lighted, someone on duty to admit delivery vans that would be arriving with milk, eggs and headless chickens from local farms. I cut across to the old wooden fence and ducked between the rails, then stood awhile, staring into the dark, aware of my breathing, sur-

prised by it, as if it were an event that only rarely and memo-
rably takes place.

I felt my way slowly along a row of trees that lined one
side of a dirt path. I moved toward the sound of traffic and
reached the highway bridge in ten or twelve minutes. The
bridge itself was closed to traffic, with repairwork in perennial progress. I stood at a point roughly midway across and
watched the cars speed below me. There was a half moon
hanging low and looking strangely submerged in the pale
mist. Traffic was steady, coming and going, pickups, hatch-
backs, vans, all carrying the question of who and where, this
early hour, and splashing the unwordable sound of their passage under the bridge.

I watched and listened, unaware of passing time, thinking
of the order and discipline of the traffic, taken for granted,
drivers maintaining a distance, fallible men and women, cars
ahead, behind, to the sides, night driving, thoughts drifting.
Why weren't there accidents every few seconds on this one
stretch of highway, even before morning rush? This is what
I thought from my position on the bridge, the surging noise
and sheer speed, the proximity of vehicles, the fundamental
differences among drivers, sex, age, language, temperament,
personal history, cars like animatronic toys, but that's flesh
and blood down there, steel and glass, and it seemed a wonder to me that they moved safely toward the mystery of their
destinations.

This is civilization, I thought, the thrust of social and
material advancement, people in motion, testing the limits
of time and space. Never mind the festering stink of burnt
fuel, the fouling of the planet. The danger may be real but
it is simply the overlay, the unavoidable veneer. What I

was seeing was also real but it had the impact of a vision, or maybe an ever-present event that flares in the observer's eye and mind as a burst of enlightenment. Look at them, whoever they are, acting in implicit accord, checking dials and numbers, showing judgment and skill, taking curves, braking gently, anticipating, watchful in three or four directions. I listened to the air blast as they passed beneath me, car after car, drivers making instantaneous decisions, news and weather on their radios, unknown worlds in their minds.

Why don't they crash all the time? The question seemed profound to me, with the first touch of dawn showing to the east. Why don't they get backended or sideswiped? It seemed inevitable from my elevated perspective—cars forced into the guardrails, nudged into lethal spins. But they just kept coming, seemingly out of nowhere, headlights, taillights, and they would be coming and going all through the budding day and into the following night.

I closed my eyes and listened. Soon I'd be going back to the camp, sinking into the everydayness of that life. Minimum security. It sounded childlike, a term of condescension and chagrin. I wanted to open my eyes to empty roads and blazing light, apocalypse, the thundering approach of something unimaginable. But minimum security was where I belonged, wasn't it? The least possible quantity, the lowest degree of restriction. Here I was, a truant, but one who would return. When I looked, finally, the mist was lifting, traffic heavier now, motorcycles, flatbeds, family cars, SUVs, drivers down there peering, the noise and rush, the compelling sense of necessity.

Who are they? Where are they going?

It occurred to me then that I was visible from the highway, a man on the bridge, at this hour, in silhouette, a man standing and watching, and it would be a natural response for the drivers, some of them, to glance up and wonder.

Who is he? What is he doing there?

He is Jerold Bradway, I thought, and he is breathing the fumes of free enterprise forever.

THE STARVELING

When it started, long before the woman, he lived in one room. He did not hope for improved circumstances. This was where he belonged, single window, shower, hotplate, a squat refrigerator parked in the bathroom, a makeshift closet for scant possessions. There is a kind of uneventfulness that resembles meditation. One morning he sat drinking coffee and staring into space when the lamp that extended from the wall rustled into flame. Faulty wiring, he thought calmly, and put out his cigarette. He watched the flames rise, the lampshade begin to bubble and melt. The memory ended here.

Now, decades later, he sat watching another woman, the one he lived with. She was at the kitchen sink, washing her cereal bowl, using a soapy bare hand to scour the edges. They were divorced now, after five or six years of marriage, still sharing an apartment, hers, a third-floor walk-up, sufficient space, sort of, tiny barking dog next door.

She was still lean, Flory, and a little lopsided, the soft brownish blond tones only now beginning to fade from her hair. One of her brassieres hung from the doorknob on the closet. He looked at it, wondering how long it had been there. It was a life that had slowly grown around them, unfailingly familiar, and there was nothing much to see that had not been seen in previous hours, days, weeks and months. The brassiere on the doorknob was a matter of months, he thought.

He sat on his cot at the other end of the narrow flat, listening to her talk idly about her new job, temporary, doing traffic reports on the radio. She was an actor, occupationally out of work, and took what came her way. Hers was the only living voice he attended to in the course of most days, an easy sort of liquid cadence with a trace of Deep South. But her broadcast voice was a power tool, all bursts and breathless medleys, and when it was possible, when he happened to be here, which was rare, during the daylight hours, he turned on the radio and listened to the all-news station where she had a narrow slot every eleven minutes, reporting on the routine havoc out there.

She spoke fantastically fast, words and key phrases expertly compressed into coded format, the accidents, road repairs, bridges and tunnels, the delays measured in geologic time. The BQE, the FDR, always the biblical Cross Bronx, ten thousand drivers with deadened eyes waiting for the gates to open, the seas to part.

He watched her approach now, slantwise, her body language of determined inquiry, head flopped left, eyes advancing through levels of scrutiny. She stopped at a distance of five feet.

"Did you get a haircut?"

He sat thinking, then reached back to run his thumb over the back of his neck. A haircut was a hurried few moments in a well-scheduled day, submitted to in order to be forgotten.

"I think so, absolutely."

"When?"

"I don't know. Maybe three days ago."

She took a step to the side, approaching once again.

"What's wrong with me? I'm just now noticing," she said. "What did he do to you?"

"Who?"

"The barber."

"I don't know. What did he do to me?"

"He emasculated your sideburns," she said.

She touched the side of his head, honoring the memory, it seemed, of what had been there, her hand still wet from the cereal bowl. Then she danced away, into a jacket and out the door. This is what they did, they came and went. She had to hurry to the studio, in midtown, and he had a movie to get to, ten-forty a.m., walking distance from here, and then another movie somewhere else, and somewhere else after that, and then one more time before his day was done.

It was a dense white summer day and there were men in orange vests jackhammering along the middle of the broad street, with concrete barriers rimming the raw crevice and every moving thing on either side taking defensive measures, taxis in stop-and-start pattern and pedestrians sprinting across the street in stages, in tactical bursts, cell phones welded to their heads.

He walked west, beginning to feel the flesh in his step, the width of chest and hips. He'd always been big, slow and strong and he was bigger and slower now, all those fistfuls of saturated fat that he pushed into his face, irresistibly, sitting slumped over the counter in diners or standing alongside food carts. He didn't eat meals, he grabbed meals, he grabbed a bite and paid and fled, and the aftertaste of whatever he absorbed lingered for hours somewhere in the lower tracts.

This was his father eating, the aging son assuming the father's spacious frame, if nothing else.

He turned north on Sixth Avenue, knowing that the theater would be near empty, three or four solitary souls. Moviegoers were souls when there were only a few of them. This was almost always the case late morning or early afternoon. They would remain solitary even as they left the theater, not exchanging a word or glance, unlike souls in the course of other kinds of witness, a remote accident or threat of nature.

He paid at the booth, got his ticket, gave it to the man in the lobby and went directly to the catacomb toilets. A few minutes later he took his seat in the small theater and waited for the feature to begin. Wait now, hurry later, these were the rules of the day. Days were all the same, movies were not.

His name was Leo Zhelezniak. It took half a lifetime before he began to fit into the name. Did he think there was a resonance in the name, or a foreignness, a history, that he could never earn? Other people lived in their names. He used to wonder whether the name itself made any difference. Maybe he would feel this separation no matter what name he carried on the plastic cards in his wallet.

He had the row to himself, seated dead center as the house went dark. Whatever moons of disquiet and melancholy hovered over his experience, recent or distant, this was the place where it might all evaporate.

Flory had ideas about his vocation. In those early years, between acting jobs, voice-overs, sales fairs and dogwalking, she occasionally joined him, three movies some days, even four, the novelty of it, the sort of inspired lunacy. A film can be undermined by the person you're seeing it with, there in the dark, a ripple effect of attitude, scene by scene, shot by shot. They both knew this. They also knew that she would do nothing to compromise the integrity of his endeavor—no whispers, nudges, bags of popcorn. But she did not overplay her sense of careful forethought. She was not a trite person. She understood that he was not turning a routine diversion into some hellish obsession.

What, then, was he doing?

She advanced theories. He was an ascetic, she said. This was one theory. She found something saintly and crazed in his undertaking, an element of self-denial, an element of penance. Sit in the dark, revere the images. Were his parents Catholic? Did his grandparents go to mass every day, before first light, in some village in the Carpathian Mountains, repeating the words of a priest with a long white beard and golden cloak? Where *were* the Carpathian Mountains? She spoke late at night, usually in bed, bodies at rest, and he liked listening to these ideas. They were impeccable fictions, with no attempt on her part to get his rendering of what might be the case. Maybe she knew it would have to be dredged out of his pores, a fever in the skin rather than a product of conscious mind.

Or he was a man escaping his past. He needed to dream away a grim memory of childhood, some misadventure of adolescence. Movies are waking dreams—daydreams, she said, protection against the recoil of that early curse, that bane. She seemed to be speaking lines from the misbegotten revival of a once-loved play. The tender sound of her voice, the make-believe she was able to unfurl, sometimes distracted Leo, who'd feel an erection beginning to hum beneath the sheets.

Was he at the movies to see a movie, she said, or maybe more narrowly, more essentially, simply to be at the movies?

He thought about this.

He could stay home and watch TV, movie after movie, on cable, three hundred channels, she said, deep into the night. He wouldn't have to get from theater to theater, subways, buses, worry, rush, and he'd be far more comfortable, he'd save himself money, he'd eat half-decent meals.

He thought about this. It was obvious, wasn't it, that there were simpler alternatives. Every alternative was simpler. A job was simpler. Dying was simpler. But he understood that her question was philosophical, not practical. She was probing his deeper recesses. Being at the movies to be at the movies. He thought about this. He owed her the gesture.

The woman entered as the feature began. He hadn't seen her in a while and was surprised to realize, only now, that he'd noted her absence. She was a recent enlistee—is that the word? He wasn't sure when she'd started showing up. She seemed awkward, slightly angular, and she was far younger than the others. There were others, the floating group of four or five people who made the circuit every day, each keeping to his or her rigid schedule, crisscrossing the city, theater to theater, mornings, nights, weekends, years.

Leo did not count himself part of the group. He did not speak to the others, ever, not a word, not a look directed their way. He saw them nonetheless, now and then, here and there, one or the other. They were vague shapes with pasty faces, planted among the lobby posters in their weary clothing, restless bearing, their postoperative posture.

He tried not to care that there were others. But how could it fail to disturb him? The sightings were unavoidable, one person at the Quad, another the next day at the Sunshine, two of them at Empire 25 in the vast rotunda or on the long steep narrow escalator that seems to lead to some high-rise form of hell.

But this was different, she was different, and he was watching her. She was seated two rows in front of him, end of the row, with the first images bringing pale light to the front of the house.

There was the long metal bar of the old police lock set into its floor niche inches from the front door. There was the tall narrow radiator, a relic, unscreened, with a pan set beneath the shutoff valve to collect the drip. At times he stared into the columns of the radiator, thinking whatever he was thinking, none of it reducible to words.

There was the cramped bathroom they shared, where his broad bottom could barely wedge itself between the tub and the wall and onto the toilet seat.

Sometimes he left his cot, by invitation, and spent the night with Flory in her bedroom, where they had wistful sex. She had a boyfriend, Avner, but said nothing about him beyond the name itself and the fact that he had a son living in Washington.

There was the photograph of her grandmother and grandfather on one wall, the kind of old family photo so drained of color and tone that it is generic, somebody's forebears, ancestors, dead relatives.

There were the notebooks crammed into the back of the closet, Leo's composition books, reminiscent of grade school, the black-and-white mottled covers, the marbled covers. These were his notes, years and miles of scrawled testimony that he'd once compiled about the movies he saw. Name of theater, title of film, starting time, running time, random thoughts on plot, principals, scenes and whatever else occurred to him—the talky teenagers seated nearby and what he said to shut them up, or the way the white subtitles disappeared into white backgrounds, stranding him with a raging argument in Korean or Farsi.

In bed with her, he sometimes flashed a thought of Avner in some dark shrouded shape-changing form, a scattered presence haunting the room.

Flory liked to punch him in the stomach, for fun. He tried to find the humor in it. Often, late, he'd come home to find her kickboxing in her pajamas. This was part of a regimen that included diet, stylized movement and lengthy meditation, her body faceup on the floor, a dish towel over her eyes. She did summer stock, gone for weeks, and sometimes, his senses dulled down, he barely knew that he was alone in the apartment.

There was his face in the mirror, gradually becoming asymmetrical, features no longer on the same axis, brows unaligned, jaw crooked, his mouth slightly aslant.

When did this begin to happen? What happens next?

They lived on nearly nothing, his wilted savings and her occasional flurries of work. They lived on habit, occupying long silences that were never tense or self-conscious. Other times, studying a playscript, she paced the floor, trying out voices, and he listened without comment. She used to give him haircuts but then stopped.

When she forgot something she wanted to tell him, she went to wherever the thought had originated, kitchen, bathroom, bedroom, and waited for it to recur.

There was a bottle of Polish vodka resting on top of the ice trays in the refrigerator. He might ignore it for three months and then, one midnight, drink sippingly and methodically from a water glass, lying back on the cot an hour later with the world all closed down, nothing left of it but a terminal throbbing ache in his forebrain.

There were the traffic reports, the sound of Flory's voice pressurized into twenty-five seconds of gridlock alerts, lane closings, emergency guardrail repairs. He sat hunched by the radio listening for hints of total global collapse in the news of a flipped vehicle on the inbound Gowanus. These reports were the Yiddish slang of everything gone wrong, reformulated in the speed diction and cool command of her delivery.

There was the fact that she'd never appeared in a movie, not as a walk-on, not in a crowd scene, and he wondered if somehow, secretly, she blamed him.

There were all the things they lived with, plain objects strangely charged with shaping their reality, things touched but not seen, or seen through.

He spent a year in college in his late twenties, working nights at the main post office on Eighth Avenue, and he took a course in philosophy that he looked forward to, week by week, page by page, mining even the footnotes in the text. Then it got hard and he stopped.

If we're not here to know what a thing is, then what is it?

There was her brassiere dangling from the doorknob on the closet.

He thought, What is it?

He left his seat while the final credits were rolling, an action he took only when the day's schedule was extremely tight. This wasn't the case today. He went out onto the avenue and stood near the curbstone. He faced the theater and waited. A man passed by, putting on lip balm, and this made Leo look up to check the position of the sun.

It wasn't long before the young woman emerged. She wore jeans tucked into dark boots and looked different in bright light, whiter, thinner, he wasn't sure. She paused for a moment, people skimming past. He thought she also looked worried and then he thought it wasn't worry but only a basic alertness to the essential details, the next showtime, the quickest way to get there. She wore a loose gray shirt and carried a shoulder bag.

Cabs went blasting past behind him.

She began to move away, long brown hair, long slow deliberate strides, tight ass in those faded jeans. He figured she was headed to the subway entrance north of here. He stood in place for an extended moment, then found himself walking in the same direction, following. Was he following? Did he need someone to tell him what he was doing? Did he need to check his position in the solar system because he'd seen a man applying sunscreen to his lips?

The next movie in his day was diagonally crosstown, up on East Eighty-sixth Street, but he could take the A train here, if the situation warranted, and then make his way across the park by bus. Built into his code of daily travel was the conviction never to take taxis. A taxi seemed like cheating, even if he wasn't sure exactly what this meant. But he knew what money meant, the tactile fact of cash leaving the hand—folding money, rubbed coins.

He moved into a trot now, already reaching for his transit card. She was still in sight, barely, among the sidewalk swarm. He had the transit card in his breast pocket, the day's slate written on an index card in the opposite pocket. He had his loose change, wallet, house keys, handkerchief, all the ordinary items that established the vital identity of his days. There was his hunger to be considered, food, soon, to steel the sorry body. He had the old Seiko wristwatch with the frayed leather band.

He paid careful attention to rain in movies. In foreign films, set in northern or eastern Europe, it seemed, sometimes, to be raining God or raining death.

Sometimes, also, he imagined himself being foreign, walking stooped and unshaven along the sides of buildings, although he didn't know why this seemed foreign. He could see himself in another life, some nameless city in Belarus or Romania. The Romanians made impressive films. Flory read movie reviews, sometimes aloud. Foreign directors were often called masters, the Taiwanese master, the Iranian master. She said you had to be a foreigner to be a master. He saw himself walking past cafés in black-and-white cities, with trolley cars going past, and lipsticked women in pretty dresses. These visions would fade in seconds but in a curious way, a serious way, they had the density of a lifetime compressed.

Flory thought he did not have to imagine an alternative life as a foreigner. He was actually leading an alternative life. In the real life, she said, he is a schoolteacher in one of the outer boroughs, a run-down neighborhood. Late one afternoon he and his colleagues get together in a local bar and describe the lives they might be living under different circumstances. Fake lives, joke lives, but on the margins of plausibility. After several drinks it is a bleary Leo who proposes the most reckless life. It is this life, his life, the movies. The others wave him off. Leo least of all, they say. The man is too earthbound, pragmatic, the most literal-minded of the bunch.

She brought the story around to their third-floor walk-up, the sight of him at the other end of the flat, seated on his cot, lacing his shoes. This is why they were still living together, she said. His stolid nature was her bedrock. She needed only what there was in plain sight, this man in body, in careless bulk, his gravitational force keeping her in balance.

Otherwise she was windblown, unfixed, eating and sleeping sporadically, never getting around to things. The rent, the phone bill, the leak, the rot, all the things you have to get around to, all the time, before they find you dead in your grandmother's nightgown. Leo did not go to the doctor but she went to the doctor because he did not. She filled prescriptions because he was here, sweeping the floor and taking out the garbage. He was not springloaded, he was safe. There was no explosion in that crouched form.

Years later people can't remember why they got married. Leo couldn't remember why they divorced. It had something to do with Flory's worldview. She dropped out of the neighborhood association, the local acting company, the volunteers for the homeless. Then she stopped voting, stopped eating meat and stopped being married. She devoted more time to her stabilization exercises, training herself to maintain difficult body positions, draped over a chair, rolled into a dense mass on the floor, a bolus, motionless for long periods, seemingly unaware of anything beyond her abdominal muscles, her vertebrae. To Leo she seemed nearly swallowed by her surroundings, on the verge of melting out of sight, dematerializing.

He watched her and thought of something he'd heard or read years earlier, in philosophy class.

All human existence is a trick of light.

He tried to recall the context of the remark. Was it about the universe and our remote and fleeting place as earthlings? Or was it something much more intimate, people in rooms, what we see and what we miss, how we pass through each other, year by year, second by second?

They'd stopped speaking to each other in meaningful ways, she said, and they'd stopped having meaningful sex.

But they needed to be here, each with the other, and he finished lacing his shoes and then stood and turned and raised the shade. The slat jutted slightly from its hem and he tried to decide whether to nudge it back into place or leave it as it was, at least for now. He remained a moment, facing the window, scarcely aware of the noise of traffic from the street.

This is where he spent part of nearly every day, ordinary rider, standing man, the subway, his back to the door. He and others, lives at pause, faces emptied out, and she as well, seated near the end of the car. He didn't have to look directly at her. There she was, head down, knees tight, upper body swiveled toward the bulkhead.

This was the midday lull between the breathless edges of

195

the rush hours but she sat as if enclosed by others and he thought she was still getting used to the subway. He thought a number of things. He thought she was a person who lived within herself, remote, elusive, whatever else. Her gaze was down and away, into nothing. He scanned the ad panels above the windows, reading the Spanish copy over and over. She had no friends, one friend. This is how he chose to define her, for now, in the early stages.

The train pulled into a station, Forty-second Street, Port Authority, and he stood away from the door and waited. She didn't move, didn't budge, and he began to imagine a crowded car, both of them standing, his body jammed against hers, pressed into her. Which way is she facing? She is facing away from him, they are front to back, bodies guided by the swerves and changing speeds, train racing past stations now, an unscheduled express.

He needed to stop thinking for a while. Or is this what everybody needed? Everybody here with eyes averted thinking about everybody else in whatever unknowable way, a total crosscurrent of feelings, wishes, dim imaginings, one second to the next.

There was a word he wanted to apply to her. It was a medical or psychological term and it took a long moment before he was able to think of it, *anorexic*, one of those words that carries its meaning with a vengeance. But it was too extreme for her. She wasn't that thin, she wasn't gaunt, she wasn't even young enough to be one, an anorectic. Did he know why he was doing this, any of it, from the instant he decided to take the wrong train, her train? There was nothing to know. It was minute-to-minute, see what's next.

Soon he was following her along the street and out of the

heat and noise of this stretch of Broadway into the cool col-
umned lobby of a major multiplex. She went past the auto-
mated ticket machines and approached the counter at the
far end of the lobby. Posters everywhere, a bare scatter of
people. She stepped onto the escalator and he understood
that he could not lose sight of her now. He rode up toward
the huge Hollywood mural and onto the carpeted second
floor. There was a man on a sofa reading a book. She went
past the video-game consoles and handed her ticket to the
woman stationed at the entrance to the theaters.

All these elements, seemingly connected, here to there,
step by step, but with no thought in his mind of a purposeful
end—just the unfixed rhythm of his need.

He stood at the access point, able to see her enter theater 6. He went back to the lobby and asked for a ticket to
whatever was showing there. The ticket seller tapped it out,
deadpan, and he headed to the escalator, walking past the
security guard whose nonchalance was probably genuine.
On the second floor again he handed the ticket to the uni-
formed woman and walked past the long food counter, veer-
ing into theater 6. Roughly two dozen heads in the semidark.
He scanned the seats and found her, fifth row, far end.

There was no satisfaction in this, having tracked her from
the end of one movie to the start of another. He felt only that
a requirement had been met, the easing of an indistinct tension. He was halfway down the side aisle when he decided
to sit directly behind her. The impulse took him by surprise
and he moved into the seat tentatively, needing to adjust to
the blatant fact of being there. Then the screen lit up and
the previews came at them like forms of laboratory torture,
in swift image and high pitch.

Their bodies were aligned, eyes aligned, his and hers. But the movie was hers, her film, her theater, and he wasn't prepared for the confusion. The movie seemed stillborn. He could not absorb what was happening. He sat with legs spread, knees braced against the seat in front of him. He was practically breathing on her and this proximity helped him work his way into things that hadn't been clear up to now. She was a woman alone. This had to be the case. She lives alone, in one room, as he did. Those were years that still gathered force in his memory, and the choice he would make, the fact of this life, scratched-out, gouged-out, first became a vision in that room. She looks down at warped floorboards. There is no bathtub, only a shower with tinny sides that rattle if you lean on them. She forgets to bathe, forgets to eat. She lies in bed, eyes open, and replays scenes from the day's films, shot by shot. She has the capacity to do this. It is natural, it is innate. She doesn't care about the actors, only the characters. They are the ones who speak, and look sadly out of windows, and die violently.

He took his eyes off the screen. Her head and shoulders, this is what he looked at, a woman who avoids contact with others, sometimes sits in her room staring at a wall. He thinks of her as a true soul, not knowing exactly what that means. Is he sure that she doesn't live with her parents? Can she manage alone? She sees certain movies many times, unlike him. She will hunt down mythical movies, those once-in-a-decade screenings. Leo saw such films only when they drifted into view. She will devote her energies to finding and seeing the elusive masterwork, damaged print, missing footage, running time eleven hours, twelve hours, nobody seems sure, a privileged act, a blessing—you travel to London, Lisbon, Prague or maybe just Brooklyn, and you sit in a crowded room and feel transformed.

Okay, he understood this. She steps away from her own shadow. She is a scant being trying to find a place to be. But there was something she had to understand. This is everyday life, this is the job, day to day. Your head is folded into a newspaper or plugged into a telephone so you can measure movie times against estimated travel times. You make the slate, keep the hours, remain true to the plan. This is what we do, he thought.

He closed his eyes for a time. He tried to see her standing naked in body profile before a mirror. She looked frail, undernourished, watching herself, half wondering who that person is. He thought about her name. He needed a name, a way to claim her, something to know her by. When he opened his eyes a house stood onscreen, alone in a wintry field. He thought of her as the Starveling. That was her name.

There was the day in Philadelphia, the day it opened, *Apocalypse Now*, over thirty years ago, the nine-twenty a.m. show, the Goldman, on Fifteenth Street. He was in town because his father had just died and he was at the movies because he could not stay away, arriving at nine sharp with a criminal's conscience, his father's death and imminent funeral serving as bookends for Brando in the jungle. His father left property to a couple of loyal friends and the money went to Leo, pretty serious money, meatpacker's money, union head's money, heavy drinker, gambler, widower, a master of graft and other amenities.

Then there was the day, decades later, when Brando died. The news came over the radio. Marlon Brando dead at eighty. It didn't make sense to Leo. Brando eighty. Brando dead made more sense than Brando eighty. It was the guy in the T-shirt or tank top who was dead, the leather jacket, not the old man with the bulging cheeks and raspy voice. Later, at the supermarket, before the first screening of the day, he expected to hear people talking about it in the checkout lines but they had other matters in mind. Do I want the olive oil spray or the canola spray? Debit or credit? He stood there thinking of his father. Two deaths forever linked, and the money, his father's bequest, was the thing that allowed him eventually to leave his job at the post office and take up the life, full-time, with Flory's encouragement.

They were just getting to know each other then. He'd already started filling notebooks with facts and commentaries, personal interpretations, and she found this fascinating. Already stacks of those schoolroom notebooks, his handwriting unreadable, half a million words, a million words, film by film, day by day, building into a cultural chronicle to be discovered a hundred years from now, one man's eccentric history of an entire era. He was a serious man. This is what she loved about Leo, she said, seated on the floor smoking dope in her underwear, with black goggles wrapped around her head. The man was gripped by a passion, a total immersion that was uncompromising, and the notebooks were solid evidence of this, objects you could clutch in your hands, words you could count, the tangible truth of a monkish dedication, and the murky handwriting only added to the wonder of the enterprise, like ancient script in a lost language.

Then he stopped.

Movies of every kind, from everywhere, maps of world imagery, and then you stop?

He stopped, he said, because the notebooks had become the reason for what he was doing. What he was doing was going to the movies. The notebooks were beginning to replace the movies. The movies didn't need the movie notes. They only needed him to be there.

Is this when she stopped cutting his hair? He wasn't sure.

He'd known from the beginning that he was advancing toward a future without paydays, holidays, birthdays, new moons, full moons, real meals or very much in the way of world news. He wanted the native act, clean, free of extraneous sensation.

He never looked at ticket sellers or ticket takers. Someone handed him a ticket, he handed it back to someone else. This stayed the same, almost everything stayed the same. But now days seemed to end an hour after they started. It was always the end of the day. The days had no names and this should not have mattered. But there was something unsettling in the anonymous week, not a sense of elemental time but of time emptied out. He walked up the stairs, near midnight, and it was here and now, night after night, that he became intensely conscious of the moment, approaching the third floor, slowing his pace, wary of rousing the neighbor's rat-faced barking dog. Another end of another day. The previous day had just ended, it seemed, at this precise place on the stairway, with the same cautious footstep, and he could see himself clearly, then and now, in midstep.

All forgotten until the following night, when the same feeling occurred, at the same place, one step from the landing.

First there was the crosstown bus and then the subway, 6 train, uptown. He thought they were headed to a theater on the Upper East Side. He also thought there had to be another word, beyond *anorexic*, that would help him see her clearly, a word invented for certain individuals to aspire to, as if they were born and raised to wrap themselves inside it.

He watched her, half a car away.

She almost never speaks. When she speaks, is there a stutter, an accent? An accent might be interesting, somewhere Scandinavian, but he decided he didn't want one. She has no telephone. She forgets to shop—food, shoes, toiletries— or simply rejects the notion. She hears voices, she hears dialogue from movies she saw as a child.

She remained in her seat when they reached Eighty-sixth Street. This made him nervous and he began to count the stops now. When he reached an even dozen the train made a leap into daylight and he found himself scanning a scene of tenements, housing projects, jagged streaks of rooftop graffiti and a river or inlet he could not identify.

She is also erratic, possibly self-destructive. There are times when she flings herself against the wall. It occurred to him that what he was doing made complete sense, to define her as someone who has taken this life, *their life*, to its predetermined limit. She has no recourse to sensible measures. She is pure, he is not. Does she forget her name? Is it possible for her to imagine the slightest semblance of well-being?

He checked the street names on the electronic route map across the aisle, dots blinking off, one by one, Whitlock, Elder, Morrison, and he began to understand where he was. He was in the Bronx, which meant he'd strayed outside the known borders. Sunlight filled the car, making him feel exposed, deprived of the cover, the protective aura he'd experienced beneath street level.

Across from him a tiny brown woman held a half-smoked cigarette, unlit. On the platform, finally, he followed the other woman, the one he was following, down to street level and along a broad avenue lined with shops, storefront offices, a Bangladeshi grocery, a Chino-Latino restaurant. He stopped noticing things and watched her walk. She seemed to be thinking each stride into physical being. They crossed the overpass of an expressway and she turned into a street of row houses with aluminum awnings. He stopped and waited for her to enter one of the houses and now the street was empty except for him.

He walked slowly back toward the train station, not knowing what to make of this. Did it contradict everything he'd come to believe about her? This street, these family homes, the difficulty she faced in getting to theaters clustered in Manhattan. In a way it made her a more compelling figure. It confirmed her determination, the depth of her calling.

She lived here because she had to live somewhere. She could not manage alone. She is staying with an older sister and her family. They are the only white family left on the block. She is the strange one, the one who never says where she is going, who rarely takes meals with the others, the one who will never marry.

Maybe there was no technical term or medical name for what she did or what she was. She just wandered on past, free of all that.

He felt the heat, Bangladeshi heat, West Indian heat. He read the names on the windows of local enterprises. This is what she sees every day, Tattoo Mayhem, Metropolitan Brace and Limb. He decided to wait within sight of the stairway to the elevated tracks. If there was a movie to come, she would show up eventually to get on the train. He ate something in Kabir's Bakery and waited, then went to Dunkin' Donuts and ate something else and waited, looking out the window. Was this the first food he'd eaten all day? Was she eating while he was eating? Did the Starveling eat?

He stood in the shadows on the corner, under the el, trains arriving and leaving, people everywhere, and he watched them, he so seldom did this, evening slowly unfolding. There was nothing here that was not ordinary but he felt compelled to examine the scene, searching for something he could not identify. Then he saw her, across the street. She was born to be unseen, he thought, except by him. She willed it, she carried it with her, the wary look and taut body, the inwardness, the void of touch. Who touched her, ever?

She wore a dark sweater now, V-neck, and there was an umbrella handle jutting from the shoulder bag.

Take the umbrella, her sister had said. Just in case.

He followed her up the stairs to the platform, same track as before, uptown, and this was another reality to absorb, that they were not headed back to Manhattan. They rode five stops to the end of the line and she went to street level and boarded a waiting bus. He felt lost and dumb, wandering blind, a passive victim of some shadowy manipulation. He also felt close to the point of breaking off contact. The bus sat there, marked Bx29. People kept boarding and after a while he followed, taking a seat near the front. Nothing happened but time seemed to be rushing past. He could see it out the window, sky darkening, things in motion. A man and woman behind him were speaking Greek. He thought the Greeks were in Queens.

Then they were moving past a landscape of parkways,

thruways, loops and interchanges, and the bus entered an enormous shopping complex, several malls, more or less contiguous, national names everywhere, franchises and megastores, a hundred soaring logos, and out there, beyond, he saw the lights and regimented shapes of a great sweep of high-rise buildings.

She nearly brushed his shoulder when she got off the bus. It wasn't until he stepped out onto the sidewalk that he realized he was standing in front of a movie theater. He stared into the transparent facade. He was ready to believe all over again. There she was inside the lobby, her sketchy body moving along the winding ticket line. He was ready to trust the moment, be himself, like a man bracingly awake after a panic dream.

He checked the display of features and starting times and bought a ticket to the film about to screen. He rode the escalator to the second level and entered theater 3. There she was at the end of a row near the front. He took a seat where he could in a crowded house and tried to think along with her, to feel what she was feeling.

Always the sense of anticipation. To look forward to, invariably, whatever the title, the story, the director, and to be able to elude the specter of disappointment. There were no disappointments, ever, not for him, not for her. They were here to be enveloped, to be transcended. Something would fly past them, reaching back to take them with it.

That was the innocent surface, on loan from childhood. There was more but what was it? It was something he'd never tried to penetrate until now, the crux of being who he was and understanding why he needed this. He sensed it in her, knew it was there, the same half life. They had no other self. They had no fake self, no veneer. They could only be the one embedded thing they were, stripped of the faces that come naturally to others. They were bare-faced, bare-souled, and maybe this is why they were here, to be safe. The world was up there, framed, on the screen, edited and corrected and bound tight, and they were here, where they belonged, in the isolated dark, being what they were, being safe.

Movies take place in the dark. This seemed an obscure truth, just now stumbled upon.

It took him a moment to realize that this was the same movie he'd seen the day before, way downtown, in Battery Park. He didn't know how to feel about this. He decided not to feel stupid. What would happen when the movie ended? This is what he ought to be thinking about.

He watched it end the same way it had ended twenty-four hours ago. She remained in her seat with people shuffling past. He did the same, waiting for her to move, a full fifteen minutes. He recognized the meaning. Movie over, no wish to leave, nothing out there but heat rising from the pavement. This is where they belonged, in a tier of empty seats, no false choices. Did he want to own her, or just touch her once, hear her speak a few words? One touch might ease the need. The place smelled of seat cushions, the dust of warm bodies.

The restrooms were at the end of a corridor. The area was clearing out when she went in that direction. He stood at the head of the corridor, thinking, trying to think. There was nothing to trust but the blank mind. Maybe he felt that he was standing watch, waiting for the other women, if there were any, to come out of the restroom. He wasn't sure what he wanted to do next and then he walked down the hall and pushed open the door. She was at the washbasin farthest from the door, splashing water in her face. The shoulder bag was at her feet. She looked up and saw him. Nothing happened, neither person moved. He drifted toward a state of neutral observation. *Neither person moved*, he thought. Then he glanced at the row of stalls, all apparently empty, doors unlatched. This was a motivated act, stark and telling, and she moved away, toward the far wall.

There were gaps in the silence, a feeling of stop and go. She was looking past him. She had the face and eyes of someone distant in time, a woman in a painting, curtains hanging in loose folds. He wanted one of them to say something.

He said, "The faucets in the men's toilet aren't working." This seemed incomplete.

"I came in here," he said, "to wash my hands."

He didn't know what would happen next. The white glare of the toilet was deathly. He felt sweat working along his shoulders and down his back. Even if she wasn't facing him directly, he was in her sightline. What would happen if she looked at him straight on, eye to eye? Is this the contact she feared, the look that triggers the action?

Neither person moved, he thought.

He nodded to her, absurdly. Her face and hands were still wet. She stood with one arm bent in front of her but it didn't seem defensive to him. She was not fending, staving off. She was just caught in midmotion, the other arm at her side, palm of hand flat against the wall.

He tried to imagine what he looked like to her, man of some size, some years, but what did he look like to anyone? He had no idea.

He felt a kind of tremor in his right arm. He thought it might begin shaking. He clenched his fist, just to see if he could do it. The thing to do was to make himself known, tell her who he was, for both of them to hear.

He said, "I keep thinking of a Japanese movie I saw about ten years ago. It was sepia tone, like grayish brown, three and a half hours plus, an afternoon screening in Times Square, theater gone now, and I can't remember the title of the movie. This should drive me crazy but it doesn't. Something happened to my memory somewhere along the way. It's because I don't sleep well. Sleep and memory are intertwined. There's a bus being hijacked, people dead, I was the only person in the theater. The theater was located down under a monster store selling CDs, DVDs, headsets, videocassettes, all kinds of audio equipment, and you go into the store and down some stairs and there's a movie theater and you buy a ticket and go in. I used to know everything about every movie I ever saw but it's all fading away. It embarrasses me to say three and a half hours. I should be talking about minutes, the exact number of minutes that make up the running time."

His voice sounded peculiar. He could hear it as though he were listening to someone else speaking. It was a steady voice, without inflection, a flat low drone.

"The lobby and theater were both deserted. Nobody anywhere. Was there a refreshment stand? This much I remember, the experience itself, alone in this place watching a movie in a language I don't understand, with subtitles, down under the street, eerie and tomblike, passengers dead, hijacker dead, driver survives, some kids survive. I used to know every title of every foreign film in English plus the original language. But my memory's shot. One thing doesn't change for you and me. We arrange the day, don't we? It's all compiled, it's organized, we make sense of it. And once we're in our seats and the feature begins, it's like something we always knew, over and over, but we can't really share it with others. Stanley Kubrick grew up in the Bronx but nowhere near where you live. Tony Curtis, the Bronx, Bernard Schwartz. I'm from Philadelphia, myself, originally. I saw *The Passenger* at Cinema Nineteen. The old memories outlive the new ones, Nineteenth Street and Chestnut. There was a huge fat man in the lobby, the one-ten show, wearing shoes with the toe caps cut away and no socks. I don't think people looked at his toes. Nobody wanted to do that. Then I came to New York and the lampshade in my room started burning. Out of nowhere, flames. I have no idea how I put out the fire. Did I throw a wet towel over the burning shade? I have no idea. Sleep and memory, these things are intertwined. But what I started to say at the beginning, the Japanese movie, I went into the men's room when it was over and the faucets didn't work. There was no water to wash my hands. That's what got me started on this whole subject. The faucets in that men's room and the faucets in this men's room. But there it made sense, there it was unreal like everything else. No people, empty refreshment stand, perfectly clean toilet, no running water. So I came in here, to wash my hands," he said.

The door behind him opened. He didn't turn to see who it was. Someone standing there, watching, witness to whatever it was that was happening here. A man in the women's toilet, that's all the witness needed to see, a man standing near the row of washbasins, a woman against the far wall.

Was the man threatening the woman against the wall? Did the man intend to approach the woman and press her to the hard tile surface, in the glaring light? The witness would also be a woman, he thought. No need to turn and look. *What would the man do to them, Witness and Starveling?* This was not a thought but a blur of mingled images, but it was also a thought, and he nearly closed his eyes to see it more clearly.

Then she was away from the wall. She took two tentative steps toward him, snatched her shoulder bag from the floor and edged quickly along the stalls and past him, around him. They were gone, both women, with Leo feeling he had a desperate second left before he went to his knees, hands to chest, everything from everywhere, a billion living minutes, all converging at this still point.

But he remained where he was, standing. He turned toward the washbasin and stared into it for a time. He ran the water and tapped the soap dispenser, washing his hands thoroughly and methodically, as if to comply with regulations. He paused again, remembering what came next, and then reached for a paper towel, and another, and one more.

The corridor was empty. There were people coming up on the escalator, a late feature about to start. He stood and watched them, trying to decide whether to stay or go.

He came in rain-soaked, climbing the stairs slowly. One step from the third landing he recalled the matching moment of the previous night, seeing himself take the step, one day's end collapsing into the other.

He entered the flat quietly and sat on the cot unlacing his shoes. Then he looked up, shoes still on, thinking something was not right. The pale fluorescent light over the kitchen sink was on, flickering, always, and he saw a shape against the far window, someone, Flory, standing motion-less. He began to speak, then stopped. She wore tights and a tank top and stood with legs together, arms raised over her head, straight up, hands clasped, palms upward. He wasn't sure whether she was looking at him. If she was looking at him, he wasn't sure whether she saw him.

He didn't move a muscle, just sat and watched. It seemed the simplest thing, a person standing in a room, a matter of stillness and balance. But as time passed the position she held began to assume a meaning, even a history, although not one he could interpret. Bare feet together, legs lightly touching at knees and thighs, the raised arms permitting a fraction of an inch of open space on either side of her head. The way the hands were entwined, the stretched body, a symmetry, a discipline that made him believe he was see-ing something in her that he'd never recognized, a truth or depth that showed him who she was. He lost all sense of time, determined to remain dead still for as long as she did, watching steadily, breathing evenly, never lapsing.

If he blinked an eye, she would disappear.

picador.com

blog
videos
interviews
extracts